Love Climbs In

Barbara Cartland

Love Climbs In

G.K. Hall & Co. • **Chivers Press**
Thorndike, Maine USA   Bath, England

This Large Print edition is published by G.K. Hall & Co., USA and by Chivers Press, England.

Published in 2001 in the U.K. by arrangement with Cartland Promotions.

Published in 2001 in the U.S. by arrangement with International Book Marketing Limited.

U.S. Softcover   0-7838-9313-2 (Paperback Series Edition)
U.K. Hardcover   0-7540-4429-7 (Chivers Large Print)
U.K. Softcover   0-7540-4430-0 (Camden Large Print)

The text of this Large Print edition is unabridged.
Other aspects of the book may vary from the original edition.

Set in 16 pt. Plantin by Al Chase.

Printed in the United States on permanent paper.

British Library Cataloguing-in-Publication Data available

Library of Congress Cataloging-in-Publication Data
Cartland, Barbara, 1902–
    Love climbs in / Barbara Cartland.
        p.   cm.
    ISBN 0-7838-9313-2 (lg. print : sc : alk. paper)
    1. Chimney sweeps — Fiction.   2. Child labor — Fiction.
3. England — Fiction.   4. Large type books.   I. Title.
PR6005.A765 L63 2001
823′.912—dc21   00-047250

AUTHOR'S NOTE

The descriptions in this novel of the tortures of the Climbing Boys is all historically factual — there was an actual case of a tiny boy of four years old who crashed down the chimney of a house in Yorkshire belonging to a family called Strickland. They found he was obviously well bred and he recognised a silver fork, saying: "Papa had forks like this."

The Stricklands learnt the boy had been stolen by a gypsy who tempted him from the garden where he was playing, to see a horse. He told them his mother was dead and his father was travelling abroad, but he was staying with his Uncle George. He had been bought from the gypsy by a Master Sweep for eight guineas.

Advertisements brought no reply, but the boy was eventually adopted by a lady who brought him up and educated him.

The Bill for the Abolition of Climbing Boys was accepted by the House of Commons in 1819, but thrown out of the House of Lords. It was not until 1875 that the country saw the last of the Climbing Boys. A Chimney Sweeper's trade card can be seen in the British Museum.

The horrors of St. Giles' persisted until 1847 when a new road was cut through it to be called

New Oxford Street. The hovels, tenements and stinking alleys were rased to the ground and the rats dispersed to a thousand different holes.

CHAPTER ONE

1817

"Captain Weyborne, M'Lord!"

The servant's voice rang out across the large Library with its richly bound books stretching from floor to ceiling.

It was a very elegant room designed by Adam, with furniture which would make any connoisseur's eyes glint.

At the far end of it the owner was lying back in a chair with one leg over the arm, a glass of champagne in his hand.

"Here you are, Freddie!" he exclaimed as the newcomer entered, "and about time!"

"I came as soon as I got your message," Freddie Weyborne replied, as he advanced over the Persian carpets towards his host. "What is the hurry?"

"Only that I wanted to talk to you before the rest of my guests get here."

Captain Weyborne accepted a glass of champagne offered to him on a silver salver by a flunkey resplendent in the Troon livery and wearing a powdered wig.

It was typical of the Marquis that he lived in the style which befitted his ancient title, even though his personal behaviour caused a number of his fellow Peers to raise their eye-brows.

7

"I cannot imagine what you want to talk to me about," Freddie Weyborne said, as the servants withdrew, "that you could not have said the day before yesterday, when I dined with you in London."

"Since then I have made a monumental decision," the Marquis replied.

He was extremely handsome, in fact his looks had made him the most admired man in London since Lord Byron had left the country.

But there was a hardness and a certain cynicism about his expression which belied the claims of those who said he was the equal of a Greek god.

He was also perilously near to being described as a Rake, and there was certainly a raffish, buccaneer expression in his eyes which women found irresistible, although his elders regarded it with suspicion.

His friend, Captain Weyborne, on the other hand was a typical type of English soldier, athletic and fresh looking, with a ready smile and a good humour which ensured that he had more friends than he could count.

The two men had been inseparable ever since they had been at Eton together and continued their education at Oxford. In that seat of learning they spent most of their time hunting, drinking and playing outrageous pranks on the other undergraduates.

They had both served with distinction in Wellington's Army but, while Captain Weyborne had remained in the Life Guards, the Marquis on his father's death had "bought himself out".

It had certainly given him more time to pursue not only the fashionable beauties of London Society, but also the "Fashionable Impures".

There was seldom a week when his escapades were not delighting the members of his Clubs but causing a frown between the eyes of mothers with eligible daughters who thought the position of Marchioness of Troon would become their offspring.

"Well, what plot are you hatching now in that overfertile brain of yours?" Freddie Weyborne asked with a smile.

"That is just what I was about to tell you," the Marquis replied, "but first things first — I have decided to get married!"

"Married?"

If he had intended to surprise his friend he had certainly succeeded, and for a moment Freddie Weyborne's mouth dropped open from sheer astonishment.

When he could get his breath he asked:

"Why, in God's name? Why?"

"Lionel has become an ardent Radical and has announced that as soon as he inherits he intends to burn down this house and make the estate into common land for anyone who wishes to use it."

"That cannot be true!" Freddie Weyborne gasped.

"I have heard it from three different sources,"

the Marquis replied, "and frankly, it does not surprise me."

Freddie Weyborne was well aware that the Marquis's younger brother Lionel, Lord Stevington, had been a bone of contention for many years.

Every family in England who possessed a second son knew how they resented the privileges that were accorded to the eldest, but few of them were as aggressive as Lionel.

Freddie had often thought it was impossible to imagine two brothers who were more dissimilar, both in character and outlook.

Lionel had a fanatical hatred of his brother and everything he stood for. He refused to use his own title and was an extreme Radical in his politics.

But it was one thing to fight against the pricks of being merely the heir presumptive to his brother and another to threaten to destroy what was one of the most outstandingly magnificent houses in Great Britain and which contained treasures that were irreplaceable.

The Troon pictures were not only the envy of every Art Gallery and Museum, but also of the Prince Regent, who had exclaimed pettishly, on several occasions to the Marquis:

"However hard I try to emulate your collection, Troon, I doubt if I shall ever equal it, even if I live to be a thousand!"

"Lionel must be only bragging," Freddie said now. "He could not seriously mean to destroy anything so unique as this house."

"I would not put it past him to set fire to it and hope that I am burnt in the conflagration," the Marquis remarked laconically.

There was nothing bitter or even angry in his voice, he was simply stating a fact.

"So you intend to beget yourself an heir," Freddie remarked dryly. "Let us hope that Lionel does not kidnap him or do away with your wife before he is actually in existence."

"I intend to keep an eye on Lionel's activities," the Marquis said. "At the same time I suppose it is time I settled down. It is what my mother has been begging me to do ever since I came of age."

"I think the Dowager is right and it is time that you took life more seriously," Freddie said with a twinkle in his eye. "After all, no-one could have sown a finer crop of wild oats than you have!"

The Marquis laughed.

"If I die by Lionel's hand it is perhaps the only epitaph that will be laid on my tomb."

"We can always add it to the medals you won for gallantry in France."

Freddie was joking, but for the moment the Marquis did not reply in the same vein.

"You know, Freddie," he said after a moment, "what I miss is the danger and excitement of war."

"It was often hellishly uncomfortable while it was taking place," Freddie replied. "I cannot forget how hungry we were that time when the food wagons did not arrive and we marched for

11

two days and nights on empty stomachs."

"All the same," the Marquis said, "we were doing something worthwhile. We were fighting the enemy and trying to out-wit them. We were using both our bodies and our brains to the very best of our ability."

A sudden thought came to Freddie's mind.

He was not as quick-witted as his friend, but although he was slower, he eventually reached the right conclusion.

"Is it because you miss the war and all its dangers," he asked, "that you have set yourself out to behave so outrageously since it ended?"

"I suppose so," the Marquis replied. "All I know is that I find peace is damned dull, and unless I can galvanize people into doing something amusing, I find myself yawning my head off."

"I have never heard such nonsense!" Freddie exclaimed. "Here you are, rolling in money, with horses any man would envy, and looks which make every 'Incomparable' fall into your arms like an over-ripe peach, and you find life dull? You are disgustingly ungrateful — that's what you are!"

"I am quite prepared to agree with you," the Marquis replied, "but the fact remains that I am bored."

"Do you think marriage will relieve your boredom?"

"I think it might even make it worse," the Marquis answered, "but it is the only thing I have not tried so far."

"And who is to be your partner in this desperate experiment?" Freddie asked sarcastically.

"Dilys — who else?"

Again for a moment Freddie seemed to be struck dumb. "Dilys?" he managed to ejaculate after some seconds had passed.

"Why not?" the Marquis asked aggressively. "She is up to snuff and every bit of mischief I suggest to her. Besides which, she makes me laugh."

There was silence and after a moment the Marquis enquired:

"Well? Have you nothing to say?"

"Not that you would want to hear," his friend answered. "Now look, Freddie, we have always been frank with each other, you and I, and we have been in some damned tough corners, one way or another. If you have any objections to Dilys as my wife, you had better say so now."

Again Freddie did not reply and after a moment the Marquis went on:

"If there is one thing that really makes me angry it is when you have that reserved, shut-in look on your face as if you could not trust yourself to speak. All right, let me know the worst. You have never approved of Dilys. You have made that pretty obvious."

"That is not true," his friend said. "I do not disapprove of her as your mistress, but a wife is a very different kettle of fish."

"In what way?"

"Oh, come on, Serle, you know as well as I do what I am trying to say. Dilys has made herself the talk of St. James's, but that is her business and not mine. But can you really see her taking your mother's place here at Troon? Or standing at the top of the stairs at Stevington House?"

Now it was the Marquis's turn not to answer, for Freddie had conjured up a picture in his mind which had often haunted him when they had been bivouacking on some barren mountainside in Portugal, or riding in the pouring rain over some wind-swept plain.

He must have been only six or seven when his Nannie had let him peep through the bannisters on the second floor of Stevington House to see his father and mother receiving a long line of guests on the floor below.

Standing at the top of the huge double staircase the Marchioness, blazing with diamonds which were almost like a crown on her fair head, had looked to her small son like a Princess who had stepped straight out of a fairy-tale.

His father resplendent in the evening clothes of a Privy Councillor with the Blue Ribbon of the Order of the Garter across his chest and his coat covered in decorations, had been almost as impressive.

His parents had stood for him at that moment for everything that was grand and at the same time stable in his life.

It was many years later, when he had watched the same picture enacted over and over again,

14

that he had thought to himself that one day he would stand in the same place and receive everyone in the land who was important or distinguished enough to enjoy his hospitality.

Yet when his father had died it had not seemed practical for him to give huge Receptions at Stevington House, and he had gradually been drawn into the raffish, carefree set of young Bucks and almost without meaning to, had become their ringleader.

After following his train of thought for some minutes he said aloud:

"That sort of life is not for me."

"Why not? Is it not inevitable that you should, some time, take up the same position in the county and in the House of Lords, that your father filled so admirably?"

"Good God, what do I know about politics?" the Marquis enquired.

"You cannot go on being the *enfant terrible* for ever."

It was the Marquis's turn to look astonished.

"Really, Freddie, this is a case of '*et tu, Brute*'! I never expected you to preach propriety! What has come over you?"

"Old age!" Freddie replied, "and that is the truth, Serle, even if you do not wish to believe it. I am getting too old to drink myself stupid every night and go on parade feeling as if I had been hit on the head by a cannon-ball."

"I know the feeling," the Marquis remarked with a twist of his lips. "Perhaps that is why I

15

intend to be married."

"An admirable resolve," Freddie said, "but not where Dilys is concerned."

"Ah! Now we are coming to the point!" the Marquis exclaimed. "Just tell me in words of not more than two syllables why Dilys will not make me the sort of wife I shall be able to tolerate."

"I have just driven her from London," Freddie replied, "and quite frankly, Serle, I do not feel like coming to fisticuffs with you. Besides, you always beat me."

"I am not going to hit you, you fool," the Marquis replied. "I would just like to hear the truth."

"All right then, if you want the truth," Freddie said, "I cannot imagine a worse fate than being married to a woman who is always looking over one's shoulder to see if someone more to her liking has just entered the room."

He looked defiantly at his friend as he spoke and saw the faint smile on the Marquis's lips.

"All right, I know exactly what you're thinking; that there would not be anyone more attractive than yourself. That may be true at the moment, but what as you grow older? What if you are ill? Do you think Dilys would sit sewing, or whatever damned thing women do, by your bedside?"

Freddie spoke with a sincerity that was unmistakable, and now the Marquis walked a little restlessly up and down the carpet.

"If it is not to be Dilys," he asked, "who is there?"

"A thousand women, all far more suitable for the position than she is!"

The Marquis went on walking and both men were thinking of the woman about whom they were speaking.

Lady Dilys Powick had startled London from the moment she became a débutante.

The daughter of the Duke of Bredon, she had the *entrée* to every important house and an invitation to every Ball and Reception that took place in the *Beau Monde.*

Six months after leaving the School-room she ran away with a penniless young man in a Foot Regiment and married him secretly.

She followed him to Portugal when his Regiment was sent there and behaved so outrageously amongst the camp followers that she was sent home.

A few months later her husband was killed in action, but she hardly bothered to give him a thought and certainly made no pretence at mourning.

She was, in fact, far too busy setting London by the ears.

Her behaviour caused her to be ostracised by all the leading hostesses, but because she was beautiful, outrageous and undoubtedly amusing, her house was invariably almost under siege from her numerous admirers.

She picked and chose her lovers in a manner which made those she refused all the more determined to enjoy her favours.

But the Marquis of Troon had been *persona grata* from the moment he appeared on Dilys's horizon, and for the last six months they had been inseparable.

She had not only taken part in all his pranks but had in many cases, instigated them and what she had said and done had lost nothing in the telling, either in the Clubs or in the *Boudoirs* of those who hated her.

To the Marquis she had been a kindred spirit, which he told himself was everything he required.

There was nothing too daring for Dilys to undertake, there was no challenge she refused, and her love-making was as satisfying and fiery as any man could desire.

As the Marquis continued pacing the carpet Freddie rose to help himself to another glass of champagne from the bottle that had been left in a large silver wine-cooler on a side-table.

"There is another thing you have forgotten, Serle," he said. "You may think I am old-fashioned, but I think it is essential to marriage."

"What is that?"

"You are obviously not in love with Dilys."

"Not in love? Then what the hell do you think I feel for her?"

"Quite a number of things which I need not enumerate," Freddie replied, walking back to the fireplace, the full glass in his hand. "But none of them are love."

"How do you know?"

"I have seen you through too many love-affairs

18

for me to number, all of which amused, fascinated, even captivated you for a time, but they were none of them love, as I think of it."

"Then what is love 'as you think of it'?" the Marquis repeated in a sarcastic voice.

"It is what my father and mother felt for each other, and what I would like to feel myself before I 'settle down'!"

"You will have to be a little more explicit than that," the Marquis said. "I knew your father and mother, and they were always very kind to me, but I never thought there was anything particular about their relationship with each other."

"It is not the sort of thing they talked about in public," Freddie said, in a slightly embarrassed voice. "But when my father died, my mother said: 'Freddie, dear, I have nothing to live for now, and all I want to do is to join your father.' She followed him four days later."

"I had no idea of that," the Marquis said after a pause. "You do not mean she killed herself?"

"No, of course not," Freddie answered. "But he was her whole life, and when he was no longer there she just gave up breathing."

"You never told me this before."

"I would not have told you now," his friend replied, "only I thought it might make you understand what I am talking about."

"I am not certain I do understand," the Marquis said, "but it is making me think."

"That is what I want you to do."

The Marquis sighed.

"Neither you nor I, Freddie, are likely to feel like that about any woman."

He paused before he went on:

"Yes, I do understand what you are trying to say to me. Of course I do! But I am not the romantic sort."

He saw the expression on his friend's face and laughed.

"All right! All right! There have been a lot of women in my life and would not pretend otherwise, some of whom have been damned attractive. Do you remember that little doe-eyed girl in Lisbon?"

The Marquis ceased speaking for a moment and then said:

"No, let us not get off the track. You are telling me that I have to feel some strange emotion I have never felt before — then I shall know that I am in love."

"That is part of it," Freddie said, "but I have a feeling there is something more."

"What do you mean by that?"

"I think that in every marriage there has to be a common ideal in the relationship, something you are aiming for together."

"What I am aiming for," the Marquis said, "is to have a son!"

"You are being deliberately obtuse. When we used to debate with each other and our friends at Oxford, you know we talked about a great many things we have not mentioned since."

"Of course we did," the Marquis agreed, "but

20

it was a lot of high-flown balderdash, analysing our souls and worrying over what happened in the next world. I have often thought we wasted a hell of a lot of time talking when we might have been chasing the pretty girls."

"You did that too," Freddie said in a tired voice. "Try to concentrate on what I am saying, Serle, because it is important."

"To me, or to you?" the Marquis asked quickly.

"To both of us, I suppose," Freddie replied. "I will tell you one thing: our friendship will never be the same if you marry Dilys."

"Why not?"

Freddie did not reply and the Marquis said slowly as if the idea had suddenly percolated his mind:

"You are not telling me — you are not saying that you — and Dilys — ?"

"That is not the sort of question you should be asking me," Freddie interrupted.

"Then you have!" the Marquis exclaimed. "Good God, I had no idea!"

"I think you will find yourself in the same uncomfortable position with a large number of your friends," Freddie said, after a moment, as if he was goaded into a reply.

The Marquis walked across to the window and looked out on the green velvet lawns stretching down to the lake lying below the house which was spanned by a stone bridge of perfect architectural proportions.

His eyes were on the swans moving slowly

21

across the silver water, but Freddie was sure he was looking with a new perception into the future, seeing a very different picture from that he had conjured up before.

There was a long silence before the Marquis said irritably:

"I cannot think, Freddie, why you should come here and upset me and try to alter the plans I have made for myself."

"If I have upset them I can only say I am sincerely glad!" Freddie remarked.

"Damn you!" the Marquis said. "There are times when I actively dislike you, and this is one of them!"

He had not turned round as he spoke and Freddie looking at the squareness of his shoulders silhouetted against the light smiled a little ruefully.

He knew that his friendship with the Marquis was far too deep and too important to both of them to be destroyed by anything.

At the same time he thought it would be more pleasant if the problem of Dilys had not been raised the moment after his arrival.

Again there was silence until as if the Marquis suddenly made up his mind, he said in a different tone:

"Anyway, the question of my marriage can be shelved for the moment, at least until after tonight."

Freddie stiffened.

"What is happening tonight?" he asked.

"Well, it was intended as a grand gesture of good-bye to my freedom, and all that sort of thing."

Freddie looked apprehensive.

"You have not already proposed to Dilys, have you?"

"No, not in actual words," the Marquis said, "but I think she is already wondering whether or not she should wear a white veil at our wedding."

Freddie let out a sound of protest.

"God Almighty, Serle!" he began, "she would be the laughing-stock . . ."

He stopped.

"You are roasting me! I might have guessed! Well, let me hear the worst. What have you planned for tonight?"

"A Midnight Steeple-Chase," the Marquis replied.

"Is that all?" Freddie questioned. "I thought it would be something new and original. I hate your steeple-chases. You always win!"

"This one is going to be different," the Marquis said, "and what is more the prizes are well worth while."

"What do you call 'worth while'?"

"A thousand guineas!"

"That will cost you nothing. You always come in first."

"Five hundred guineas to the second and a hundred for third place."

"That gives somebody a sporting chance," Freddie admitted. "But what is so original about a Midnight Steeple-Chase? You have had them before. Your last one left my best horse lame for a month."

"You should be a better rider," the Marquis retorted, "and tonight you will have to be."

"Why?"

"I intend introducing certain handicaps."

Freddie groaned.

"I knew there was going to be something dangerous about it, in which case I am not going to take part."

"Can you really be so chicken-livered?" the Marquis jeered.

"Certainly!" his friend replied. "I consider my life too valuable to throw it away on some school-boy's taunt of: 'I ride better than you!' You should grow up, Serle."

"I will call you out if you talk to me like that," the Marquis said. "This will be a race for grown-ups, I assure you."

"If you think I am going to ride in my night-shirt with my eyes bandaged or sitting backwards in the saddle you can count me out!" Freddie retorted. "My father always said the Steeple-Chases were for fools who want to risk their necks, and the more foolish of them end up in the Church-yard. That is where I have no wish to be at the moment."

"Stop being a spoil-sport, Freddie!" the Marquis ordered. "Whether you take part or not there will be at least twenty competitors because they have already accepted."

"So you have been planning this nonsense for a long time."

"For the last three days since I decided to get married," the Marquis replied. "I told myself if I survived the Steeple-Chase, then I could survive marriage. It seemed there was nothing much to choose between them except that the Steeple-Chase would undoubtedly be more enjoyable."

"The truth is you are seeking danger," Freddie said. "Now tell me what the conditions are which make this particular Chase unique."

"I thought it would be amusing," the Marquis said slowly, as if he was choosing his words, "if every contestant rode as if he only had one arm and one eye. It is damned difficult, as it happens, to see with one eye when you are used to using two."

"And that means," Freddie said, "you will find it hard to take your fences and undoubtedly break your neck! It is too big a gamble. I will be the referee and use two eyes."

"Forsett has already agreed to do that," the Marquis replied. "He disapproves, but at the same time, he is completely just and everyone will accept his decision should there be any controversy."

Freddie knew this was true where Lord Forsett was concerned.

He was older than the Marquis and himself, and he had been too badly wounded in battle to be able to race his horses or to walk without a stick.

They all respected him as a brave man and it was true that whatever decision he made, they would accept.

"Forsett or no Forsett," Freddie said, "I only hope you have ordered plenty of stretcher-bearers to pick up the casualties and Surgeons to set broken arms and legs, besides grave-diggers to bury those who fall on their heads!"

"Stop being so gloomy," the Marquis commanded, "we are going to have the best dinner we have ever had. The wines will be superlative — the finest I have in the cellar. After that the majority of those present will be only too glad to compete for the prizes I am offering."

"That I can well believe," Freddie remarked, "but the more sensible of your friends will undoubtedly have an excuse which will prevent them from accepting your invitation. Who is coming?"

The Marquis gave him a rapid list of names, most of whom he knew well. Then as he added: 'Sir Charles Lingfield', Freddie repeated:

"Lingfield? But he is too old!"

"Not really. I do not suppose he has reached his fortieth birthday."

"Then he *is* too old," Freddie protested. "You know as well as I do, Serle, that if the course is the same as we have ridden over on previous occasions the jumps are very steep for men of our age, let alone an older man."

"I like Lingfield, and his house is on my estate. I can hardly leave him out."

"If he had any sense he would refuse."

"Well, he has accepted," the Marquis said, "so what do you expect me to do? Say: 'Freddie thinks you are too old, so run home, my dear man, and come another day when things are easier'?"

"I suppose it is all right," Freddie said reluctantly. "I have seen Lingfield out hunting, he is a good rider."

"Then stop clucking over my guests like a mother-hen," the Marquis ordered. "Nobody is going to get hurt. If the course is too rough for them they can always pull off their eye-shade and unstrap their arm. It is as easy as that."

"I hope you are right," Freddie said disparagingly. "Personally, I think it all sounds like an unnecessary risk of life and limb to make a Roman holiday."

"Is that what you consider I am doing?"

"Of course you are! You are bringing in the sacrificial animals and a few Christians to amuse yourself, and personally I think it is all quite unnecessary."

The Marquis poured himself out another glass of champagne.

"What I would really like at the moment," he said, "is to have a call from Wellington to say he needs us both. I would like to shake the creases out of my uniform and ride off with you to the nearest Barracks, knowing there was an adventure ahead and that we would both be far too excited to suffer one moment of boredom."

27

"I know what you meant," Freddie said after a moment. "At the same time, I think we have to face the fact that we have to come to terms with a world without war. Personally, I am quite content as I am. I can find many amusements in London. I am looking forward both to the shooting and hunting in the autumn."

"One small fox," the Marquis said disparagingly.

"Did you really enjoy killing Frenchmen?" Freddie enquired.

There was a moment's pause before the Marquis replied:

"No, it was the chase that I liked. It was exhilarating, but I never wanted to think of the result of the objective."

"That is what I felt too," Freddie said. "I could not help remembering a great deal of the time that the French were men like us; ordinary men with a life to live, and perhaps, and this I could not bear to think about — a wife and children waiting for them somewhere far away in France."

"Are you insinuating that there is something wrong with me," the Marquis asked, "because I want to go on fighting?"

"No, I do not think it is that you want to go on fighting," Freddie replied. "It is the excitement and the danger you enjoy, and that is a very different thing."

The Marquis smiled triumphantly.

"That is exactly what I am giving you tonight."

"Oh, to hell with you!" Freddie explained irritably. "You always beat me in an argument. All right — you win! I will ride in your blasted Steeple-Chase, and I only hope that tomorrow my head is still on my body and you are not weeping beside my coffin."

"I think it is very unlikely that I shall be doing that," the Marquis said, "and although it has been a hard battle to get you to participate in my race, all I can say is that I should have been very disappointed if you had really been adamant about not taking part."

The Butler had glanced twice at the clock on the mantelpiece before the door opened and Freddie came slowly and a trifle unsteadily into the Breakfast-Room.

As he reached the table a footman hurried to pull out a chair for him and another placed a white linen napkin on his knees while a third went to the sideboard where a large array of crested silver dishes reposed on tripods beneath which burned oil soaked wicks with which to keep them warm.

However before the dishes could be carried to Freddie's side for his inspection, he merely grunted in a hoarse voice which seemed somehow to be constricted in his throat:

"Brandy! What I need is brandy!"

"Of course, Sir."

The Butler made a gesture with his hand and the silver dishes were put back over the burning wicks as a footman hurried forward with a cut-glass decanter from which he poured brandy into a glass at Freddie's side.

Before he could raise the glass to his lips the door opened and the Marquis walked in.

"Good-morning, Freddie!" he said, and as his friend did not answer he said: "You look somewhat the worse for wear."

Freddie merely groaned as the Marquis went to the sideboard where the footman raised the lids of the silver dishes so that he could inspect what was inside.

"I will have a lamb chop," he said finally and sat down at the table.

There was a smile on his lips as he looked at Freddie's pale face and the manner in which by now his elbow was on the table and his forehead was resting on his hand.

He waited until a lamb chop had been placed in front of him and the Butler had poured him a cup of coffee before he said:

"The trouble with you, Freddie, is that you mix your drinks. I noticed last night that you drank a considerable amount of port, while I followed the champagne with a very little brandy. It is always wisest to keep off red wines when one is riding."

Whatever he had drunk it certainly did not seem to have affected the Marquis's good looks, and the exercise of the night did not seem to have in any way diminished his usual vitality.

"It is not only what I drank," Freddie said

after a moment. "It is that I am damned stiff, and my arm feels almost paralysed through having been strapped down for so long."

"You must have let them tie it too tightly," the Marquis remarked without much feeling. "As a matter of fact, Freddie, I thought you rode exceedingly well. It was just bad luck that Lingfield pipped you for second place. But at least you have come away with a hundred guineas to your credit."

"I would gladly pay more not to feel as I do now," Freddie replied.

The Marquis laughed.

"You will soon be better. Have something to eat. There is nothing worse than alcohol on an empty stomach."

"Leave me alone," Freddie said. "I know what is best for me."

"Very well," the Marquis answered. "Be it on your own head, but quite frankly I thought last night was a tremendous success. The dinner was excellent, you must admit that."

Freddie murmured something which was inaudible and the Marquis continued:

"You cannot deny that it was a triumph that only three riders failed to complete the course and not because they hurt themselves either. Bingham's horse went lame and so did Henderson's. Ironside fell at the water-jump which was not surprising. I have never thought much of his horses, although he boasts about them."

Freddie took another sip of brandy, then he said:

"You are right, Serle, it is my own fault. I feel as if my head is going to crack open. I should not have drunk the port and certainly not the claret we drank when we got back here."

"You will live and learn," the Marquis said. "I suppose it has never struck you that the reason why I win my own Steeple-Chases is that I am a damned sight more abstemious than the rest of the riders."

There was a somewhat wry smile on Freddie's face as he said:

"So to make sure of your success you tempt your guests like a Siren with all the delicacies which you feel they will not be able to refuse."

"That is, in fact, the first fence," the Marquis replied.

Freddie laughed as if he could not help himself.

"Really, Serle, you are incorrigible! I suppose I should accuse you of cheating."

"It is not cheating," the Marquis replied. "It is just using my brains and taking advantage of another fellow's stupidity. You know I never drink a lot when I am going hunting nor did I before a battle."

"That is true, now I come to think of it," Freddie admitted. "You were always in the prime of condition while a great number of fellows poured that filthy wine which was the best we could get, down their throats. I think really they were giving themselves 'Dutch courage'."

"Exactly!" the Marquis agreed.

He finished his coffee and the Butler hurried to his side with the silver coffee-pot.

As he did so the door opened and a man came into the room.

"Good-morning, Chamberlain!" the Marquis said. "Freddie, you have not seen Graham Chamberlain since you arrived."

"No," Freddie agreed. "How are you, Chamberlain? Nice to see you again."

"Delightful to see you, Captain," Mr. Chamberlain replied.

He was a man of thirty-seven and he had served in the same Regiment as the Marquis and Freddie.

On his accession the Marquis had retired his father's Comptroller who was far too old to carry on and remembered a very intelligent and active officer in charge of Ordnance.

When it was suggested to him that there was a job which might be to his liking if he was thinking of leaving the Regiment, Lieutenant Graham Chamberlain, who had little chance of preferment, was only too delighted to accept it.

The Marquis prided himself, and he rarely made a mistake, on choosing the right man for the right job, and where Mr. Chamberlain was concerned that was certainly true.

He had taken over his new position with an enthusiasm which was only echoed by his commonsense and the knowledge that his Army training stood him in good stead.

Within six months he had swept away a lot of unnecessary extravagances, tightened up the administration of all the Marquis's houses, and in a gratifying manner, gained the respect of those with whom he worked.

"The race was a great success, Chamberlain," the Marquis said now.

"So I have heard, My Lord, but I am afraid I have bad news."

"Bad news?" the Marquis asked.

"Yes, Sir Charles Lingfield is dead."

"Dead?" the Marquis ejaculated. "But that is impossible! When he left here he was perfectly well and delighted at having won second prize. I saw him to the door myself."

"He had a heart-attack on the way home, My Lord, and was found early this morning at the far end of the Park, before he could reach his own house."

"I am extremely sorry about that."

"So am I," Freddie interposed. "I liked Lingfield. He was a decent chap, and I should imagine he was a good soldier."

"I am sure he was," the Marquis said. "Will you convey, Chamberlain, my condolences and sympathies to his widow?"

"Lady Lingfield died several years ago, My Lord. But he has a daughter. I know that she will be very distressed by her father's death."

"Then convey my condolences to her," the Marquis said, "and of course, send a wreath. I suppose he will be buried in the village Church-yard?"

"I imagine so, My Lord, but there is something else." The Marquis glanced up from the table at his Comptroller.

"No more casualties, I hope?"

"No, My Lord, but you will remember last night that you, I think jokingly, told anyone who was apprehensive about the ride ahead, to make a will."

"It was a joke," the Marquis said, "and some of the wills I read were certainly amusing."

He smiled thinking of how one man had left him a pack of fox-hounds with the proviso that every year they should be given a barrel of beer when the anniversary of their past owner's death came round.

"Do your fox-hounds drink beer, Guy?" he had enquired.

"That's what I want you to find out, ol' boy," the writer of the will replied.

The Marquis had learnt by the slur in his voice and the manner in which he spoke that he was in fact, 'foxed'.

Another will left him a collection of stuffed birds with the instruction that they should decorate the most appropriate room in his house.

Several suggestions were offered to which this room might be, and others of the diners had striven to produce even more outrageous bequests with the terms of which they averred their host would be obliged to comply.

"Are you telling me," the Marquis asked now, "that Lingfield made a will last night?"

"Yes, he did, My Lord, and what is more, he had it witnessed."

There was something in the way his Comptroller spoke which made the Marquis glance at him sharply.

"You are making me curious," he said. "What does this will contain?"

"Sir Charles, My Lord, appointed you the Guardian of his daughter."

"The Guardian of his daughter?" the Marquis repeated incredulously.

"Yes, My Lord, and I must inform Your Lordship that I consider the document in question to be completely legal!"

CHAPTER TWO

Valeta looked helplessly around the small but attractive Drawing-Room which she always felt had never been the same since her mother died.

It was a room that was very 'lived in', and therefore contained an accumulation of treasures which had been collected over many years.

There were not only pieces of china that had come from her mother's old home, but there were also small objects that Valeta had either made or bought for her parents as gifts for birthdays and Christmas.

There was also a number of skilfully executed water colours, some framed, some unframed, and a number of silhouettes which Valeta had cut out and had quite a professional touch about them.

Besides these there were books not only in the elegant Chippendale bookcase, but because it was over-full, piled on tables and even chairs that were not often used.

Valeta looked around and knew that, if the Drawing-Room was full of a hundred things she could not bear to part with, her father's Study was worse.

Because he like her mother, enjoyed reading, in that room too there were books everywhere, piled high on the floor, on the chairs, on tables, and however hard she tried to keep the room tidy it was a sheer impossibility.

"How could I leave here?" Valeta asked her-self, "and if I did, where would I go?"

She knew that every room in the house was a part of herself and while common sense told her that now her father was dead she could not afford to go on living at the Manor, there was no answer to the question — where else could she go?

She had already discussed it with her old Nanny who had been with her ever since she was born and who had said in no uncertain terms that she was too old at her age to move about.

"But, Nanny, we cannot stay here."

"Why not?"

"Because we have to pay the rent and you know as well as I do, that without Papa's pension, we will not have enough to live on."

"If His Lordship has any decency about him, which I rather doubt," Nanny retorted, "then he'll charge you nothing to live here, considering it's his fault with his wild ideas that your father's not alive today."

Nanny had said this over and over again and because Valeta felt she could not bear it any more, she had gone from the kitchen to hide the tears in her eyes.

"Oh, Papa," she whispered when she took refuge in his Study, "how can I live without you? What shall I do now there is no-one to laugh with or talk to?"

Because she knew her father had always hated

women to cry, she fought back the tears that came to her eyes and walked to the window to look out through the diamond-paned casement onto the garden.

It was ablaze with flowers because both her father and mother had enjoyed working in it, while old Jake had quite enough to do in growing vegetables and potatoes for the house without wasting his time on what he called 'them there flowers'.

It had been hard enough to keep her father happy, Valeta thought, after her mother had died, but because she had loved him they had somehow managed to hide from each other the ache that was always in their hearts and the inescapable feeling that something very vital was missing from both their lives.

"Now I am alone," Valeta told herself, and she knew she had to face it with the courage that had been so characteristic of her father.

He had not only been outstandingly brave when he was in the Army, but he had the courage which made him face every vicissitude of life with his head high and a determination that he would never be personally defeated by adversity.

"He died because he was brave," Valeta whispered and once again had to fight back the tears that flooded into her eyes.

She had only just managed to control them when she heard the door open and Nanny say in what Valeta knew was her disapproving voice:

"The Marquis of Troon has called to see you!"

"The Marquis?" Valeta repeated.

"And not before it's time!" Nanny said tartly. "If you asks me he should have paid you a visit before now to express his condolences."

Valeta was not listening.

She was smoothing down the skirts of her gown and patting her hair into place.

Then with an expression on her face which Nanny did not recognise she walked from the Study and across the small hall to the Drawing-Room.

When she reached the door she drew a deep breath as if she felt it gave her something she needed, then turned the handle.

The Marquis was standing at one of the bow-windows looking out, as Valeta had done a few minutes earlier, onto the garden.

He was, in fact, thinking how attractive it was with the sun-dial in the centre and beds of roses radiating out from it like the dial of a clock.

There was honeysuckle climbing over the roof of a small arbour and the flowers around it were planted so as to form great clumps of vivid colour that would have been the delight of any artist's eye.

As he heard someone come into the room the Marquis turned round and at first glance at Valeta, was astonished at her appearance.

Because Sir Charles had been a good-looking man he somehow had expected that his daughter would be attractive, but he had certainly not imagined she would be a beauty.

40

The girl he saw standing just inside the room had a small heart-shaped face which seemed to be filled with two large grey eyes fringed with dark lashes.

Her skin had the translucence of the finest porcelain and her hair, which was very fair, had golden lights in it which seemed to reflect the sunshine outside.

He thought she might have been dressed in black, but instead she was wearing a white muslin gown of what his expert eye recognised was a cheap material but which clung to her figure making her look like a Greek goddess come to life.

The only concession to her bereavement were two narrow ribbons of black velvet which had obviously been added recently to the gown and which outlined her small breasts.

For a moment neither the Marquis nor Valeta spoke. Then in a low voice she said:

"You wished to see me, My Lord?"

She made a small curtsey as she spoke and moved slowly towards the fireplace and the Marquis followed her.

She stood waiting but did not invite him to sit down. Instead there was a look on her face he did not at first understand.

"I have called, Miss Lingfield," he said, "to express my very deep sympathy on your father's unfortunate death. I hope you read the card I attached to the wreath I sent to his funeral last week."

Valeta did not speak, she merely made a slight inclination of her head.

There was a pause and it was obvious the Marquis waited for some comment. As none came he continued:

"I have not called earlier because I felt it only right to give you time to get over the first shock of your loss, but now I feel there are certain things we should discuss."

"I presume, My Lord, you are referring to the rent."

The Marquis raised his eye-brows.

"Actually that had not entered my mind. I came to ask you first why you returned the five hundred guineas your father won at the Steeple-Chase."

Again there was silence, then as if she knew she must answer this question, Valeta said:

"You surely do not expect me to accept money which was the cause of my father losing his life!"

"I was afraid that might be your attitude," the Marquis replied, "although I was hoping you would not attribute your father's death to the race in which he rode magnificently."

He hesitated a moment before he said:

"I am informed by Dr. Moorland that your father had, in fact, suffered from heart trouble for some time."

"That is true," Valeta answered. "Dr. Moorland must also have informed Your Lordship that my father had been told not to exert himself unduly or place any unnatural strain upon his heart."

"In which case surely it was unwise to ride in a Steeple-Chase?" the Marquis ventured.

"Very unwise," Valeta agreed.

There was a note in her voice which made the Marquis say:

"I can understand that your father's sporting instincts overcame his sense of caution, but you can hardly hold me responsible."

"Who else?" Valeta enquired.

Then before the Marquis could speak she said:

"I suppose it has never struck you when thinking up some nonsensical amusement to pass the time that men like my father might risk their lives because they needed the prize-money?"

Valeta's tone was now scathing and the Marquis realised the expression on her face which he had not at first understood was one both of anger and contempt.

He was not used to having women, especially beautiful ones, looking at him in such a manner and for the moment he was nonplussed.

Then he said:

"I think that is an unfair accusation."

"It is the truth, My Lord," Valeta replied. "My father would be alive today if you had not offered such large money prizes for what I consider a degrading spectacle of grown men making fools of themselves."

"So that is what you think of my Steeple-Chase!" the Marquis remarked.

"It is!" Valeta replied, "it also applies to the

others you have organised and which have been the talk of the neighbourhood and, if you want the truth, set a bad example to those who work on the Troon estate."

This was plain speaking and the Marquis thought that never in his life had a woman spoken to him in such a manner.

It was all the more wounding to his pride because Valeta was not only so lovely but so young, and for a moment he found himself almost speechless. Then he said with an effort at dignity:

"I am not in the habit of defending my actions to anyone, and I think we have other things we should discuss, Miss Lingfield, which are more important to you personally."

"I cannot imagine anything more important than the fact that my father has been killed through sheer stupidity," Valeta said. "And now perhaps you understand why I would not take the 'blood money' that was brought to me and which I considered in the circumstances to be an insult!"

"That is a very foolish attitude!" the Marquis said firmly. "You told me that your father rode in the race because he needed the money. He won the second prize riding, as I have already said, magnificently, and knowing Sir Charles in the past I am quite certain he enjoyed every minute of it."

He glanced around the room before he added:

"You need the money and it would therefore

be absurd not to accept the five hundred guineas. However, as it happens that is not important."

"Nothing you can say will alter my decision, My Lord," Valeta answered, "but what is important is that, while I wish to stay on here in my home, since my father's pension died with him I cannot afford it unless Your Lordship will reduce the rent."

"The rent for the houses on my estate is not something I attend to personally," the Marquis replied.

"Then you should do!" Valeta answered. "I presume you realise that your tenant-farmers for instance, are finding it very hard to pay their rents, and I understand . . ."

She stopped.

The Marquis guessed she had intended once again to be rude, then thought better of it.

"If my farmers find their rents excessive," he said in an icy voice which would have made most of his acquaintances feel uncomfortable, "they are always at liberty to speak to my Agent."

"Your Agent, My Lord, can hardly be generous with your money unless you give him the authority to do so."

The Marquis gave a sigh of exasperation.

"Really, Miss Lingfield, I cannot see that this conversation is leading us anywhere. My rents are not a matter that should concern you."

"They should certainly concern you, My Lord!" Valeta replied. "Living in the depths of the country we still hear of your extravagances in London, the parties at which money is thrown away as it was thrown away on the grotesque spectacle of grown men behaving like clowns. I can only suppose that you are not aware that the agricultural community after the harvest failed last year, are reduced to praying that by some miracle they can survive this."

She made a little sound that was almost a sob as she said:

"Have you any idea what it is like, when you have nothing to live on but hope, to watch someone like Your Lordship throwing money away in such a profligate manner?"

She spoke aggressively, but because her voice was soft and musical and the lips that uttered the words were sweetly curved the Marquis surprisingly did not fly into a rage.

Instead deliberately he sat down in an arm-chair and crossed his legs.

"When I came here, Miss Lingfield," he said, "it was to talk about you. We seem to have diverged very far from the subject in question."

"There is no need for you to interest yourself in me, My Lord," Valeta replied, "except where it concerns the rent of this house."

"That is not true," the Marquis said. "I am, in fact, vitally concerned with your well-being."

"If that is because you feel responsible for Papa's death it is quite unnecessary."

"I consider it very necessary," the Marquis argued. "After all you are very young, and I am

46

interested to know what you intend to do now you are alone in the world. Have you any relations with whom you could live?"

"That is my business, My Lord, but I would like to remain here."

"Alone?"

The Marquis's question seemed to ring out.

Valeta lifted her chin a little higher as if she longed to tell him to mind his own business.

Then as he was obviously waiting for her answer she replied slowly:

"I have my old Nurse with me who has looked after me since I was a baby. We will manage, one way or another."

"What does that mean?" the Marquis asked bluntly.

"We can grow a great deal of what we need to eat," Valeta replied, "and perhaps I can earn a little money."

"How?"

There was silence and he had the feeling she was not going to answer him.

"I want to know," he said after a second or two.

"Why?"

"Because, as it happens, I have a right to know!"

"A right?"

"That is another reason why I came to see you," the Marquis said. "Before your father left my house on the night of the race he made a Will."

"A Will?"

There was no doubt that Valeta was astonished.

"Some of my guests," the Marquis explained, "made Wills as a joke, but your father made his in all seriousness, and what is more, it was witnessed by the men sitting on either side of him at dinner!"

Valeta was looking at him suspiciously as if she did not really believe what he was telling her. Then she asked:

"What . . . did this Will . . . contain?"

"It appointed me your Guardian until you married or reached the age of twenty-five."

Although the Marquis had seated himself Valeta had remained standing.

Now, as if she felt her legs would not support her, she sat down on a chair opposite him and her eyes fixed on him seemed almost to double in size.

"My . . . Guardian?" she murmured beneath her breath. "You can therefore understand," the Marquis said, "why I think I have a right to be concerned in your future."

"You cannot take this . . . seriously?" Valeta said. "My father, I think, made a Will which was deposited with his Solicitors and which left me everything he possessed."

"Which I gather," the Marquis remarked dryly, "is not very much."

"It is all I need," Valeta said defiantly.

"That is not true because if it was sufficient for your needs you would not need a reduction in your rent."

His logic was inescapable and Valeta said:

"What I want, My Lord, is to continue to live here and be left alone."

"I should have thought it was a somewhat unnatural life and a very uninspired ambition for a young woman."

"It is what I want to do."

The Marquis leaned back a little further in his chair. "The question is," he said, "whether I will allow you to do it."

If he had meant to be provocative he succeeded and he saw the flash of anger in Valeta's eyes.

He thought with a feeling of amusement that at least he was getting his own back for her rudeness, and after a moment in a very much smaller voice she said:

"Could you . . . really prevent me from . . . doing anything I . . . want?"

"I am assured that your father's Will is legal," the Marquis said, "in which case, as your Guardian, I am responsible for you, and if you went to the Courts I think you would find that you had to obey me."

Valeta thought for a moment, then she said:

"The best thing that can possibly happen, My Lord, is to forget this absurd Will which my father made obviously after he had enjoyed a very good dinner."

The Marquis did not miss the inference Valeta was making that her father had been under the influence of alcohol and he asked bluntly:

"Did your father often drink to excess?"

"No, of course not!" Valeta replied hotly. "He was very abstemious, and always so before he rode in a race."

The Marquis smiled.

"In which case your father obviously intended his Will to be taken seriously because he thought he was doing the best thing for you. What is more, he could have had a premonition of what might happen to him."

He thought as he spoke that he had made a point, and felt almost as if he had been arguing with Freddie and, as they would have said to each other: — "That is Round One to you!"

Valeta was silent for a moment, then she said:

"You cannot really wish to . . . concern yourself with . . . me?"

"Naturally I am finding it rather a nuisance," the Marquis answered loftily, "but it is obviously my duty to carry out your father's last wishes."

"I should like to see this Will before I am convinced that it is in fact, valid."

"Mr. Chamberlain, my Comptroller, will show it to you any time if you would like to call at the house," the Marquis replied, "but as several people saw your father writing it and two eminently respectable gentlemen witnessed his signature, I think you would find it very difficult to prove it was a forgery or invalid."

Again Valeta was silent and now she looked down at her linked hands as if she was striving to find something with which to confront the Marquis.

As he looked at her bent head he was aware how long and dark were her lashes against the pale skin.

The sunshine coming through the window seemed to dance on her hair, which though it was not fashionably dressed, was the Marquis thought, a more attractive colour than he had seen for a very long time.

On an impulse he bent forward in his chair.

"Suppose, Miss Lingfield," he said in a tone which most women found irresistible, "we stop duelling with each other and get down to hard facts."

She glanced at him and he knew by the expression in her eyes that she was still hating him, but he went on:

"You have no wish to be my Ward and, I assure you, I did not seek the post as your Guardian. But I will certainly try to make it as easy as possible for us both if we can co-operate over the matter."

"In . . . what way?"

"Shall we start with the problem of your future?"

"I have told you that I want to stay here, with my Nurse."

"I think that might be possible for the time being until we can find you a suitable Chaperon."

Valeta stiffened.

"A Chaperon?" she repeated. "Why should I need a Chaperon?"

"I should have thought that was obvious," the Marquis replied. "It is not usual for an attractive young woman of your age to live alone with only a servant to keep her company."

"Nanny is more than that!"

"She was an employee of your father and mother's."

Valeta pressed her lips together.

"I do not want a Chaperon!"

"I cannot believe you would want to be the subject of ill-natured gossip."

She made a little gesture with her hands, then smiled.

"There are not many people who are likely to talk about me. My neighbours who were fond of my father and mother will, I am sure, quite understand my predicament at having lost them both and will not be inclined to be critical."

"That might have been true in other circumstances."

He saw that Valeta did not understand and explained, choosing his words with care:

"You are my tenant, but I am also your Guardian!"

For a moment the implication of what he had said did not penetrate Valeta's mind. Then for the first time since he had entered the room, she realised he was a young and handsome man and the colour swept into her pale cheeks.

After a moment she said in a hesitating voice:

"I . . . I suppose you could not . . . tear up Papa's . . . Will and just . . . forget about it?"

"That might have been possible if I was the only person who knew he had written it."

Valeta looked down again at her hands.

"What do you . . . want me to . . . do?" she asked.

"I want you to stay here for the moment," the Marquis said, "and think if you have any relative or friend who could come and live with you. If not, I suppose I must find someone."

He knew as he spoke, that this was a very unlikely contingency.

In the smart, pleasure-seeking, rather raffish Society in which he moved in London there was certainly no woman who would wish to bury herself in the country in a small unimportant Manor house.

As if his thoughts communicated themselves to Valeta, after a moment she said:

"I will try and think of someone . . . I promise you . . . because I want so much to . . . stay here."

"Most girls of your age," the Marquis said, "would want to be in London, meeting eligible gentlemen to whom they might be married."

"That is . . . impossible where I am concerned."

"Why?" the Marquis enquired.

"Because I cannot . . . afford to live in London," Valeta replied as if speaking to a rather stupid child.

"No, I can understand that," the Marquis

agreed, "but perhaps something could be arranged."

Her eyes widened and she asked:

"What do you . . . mean by that?"

"I was just thinking," the Marquis replied, "that as your Guardian I ought perhaps to find someone who would introduce you to the fashionable world."

"That will be quite unnecessary," Valeta answered. "I have already told you that I want to stay here. I would like to make this quite clear: even if you are my Guardian I will not accept anything from you, nor will I ever forgive you for being responsible for my father's death."

The anger was back in her voice and because the Marquis could never resist a fight he retorted:

"That, if I may say so, is a very stupid attitude. You know as well as I do that your father was warned not to exert himself unnecessarily, and he must have known the consequences of riding in a very gruelling Steeple-Chase in which most of the riders were years younger than he was!"

"I can quite see," Valeta replied, "that you are trying to exonerate yourself from all blame, but when people are tempted beyond endurance we blame the Devil, not the temptation!"

"So that is how you think of me," the Marquis said.

"You can hardly expect me to think anything else," Valeta retorted, "and this is not the first time you have tempted men into injuring themselves simply, I suppose, so that you can wile away an idle hour."

"To whom are you referring this time?" the Marquis enquired.

"A young man who was not a particularly good rider broke his leg in the last Steeple-Chase you arranged," Valeta replied, "and he is still partially crippled."

"Who was that?"

"Nigel Stone."

"The General's son?"

"Yes."

"I knew he had broken his leg, but I had no idea that he was not restored to health."

"I expect those who participate in your 'fun' are easily forgotten, once the Circus is over."

The Marquis looked at her, then said slowly:

"You have a very unusual way of saying what you think, Miss Lingfield. Perhaps you are wise to bury yourself in the country. Such frankness might cause a furore anywhere else."

He thought that once again he had scored a point, but Valeta replied in what he knew was a deliberately demure voice:

"Papa always said that when a contestant resorts to personal abuse it means he has lost the argument."

Unexpectedly the Marquis found himself laughing, and saw as he did so, that Valeta was looking at him in surprise.

"I came here," he said after a moment, "expecting after I had offered you my sympathy and condolences to have to wipe away your tears and that you would be grateful for any generosity I could show you in the future. I find I am mistaken."

"Very mistaken, My Lord! As I have already said I have no intention of accepting anything that you might give me."

"I should not be too sure of that," the Marquis said. "As I have already pointed out, as your Guardian you legally have to obey me."

As he spoke he saw Valeta put up her chin and make a little movement as if she would have tossed her head.

He told himself that the interview had certainly been unexpected, and in a way more amusing than he had thought possible.

Now he was no longer angry he found it incredible that this small, lovely creature should defy him and look at him with a violent hatred in her expression that he had never before known — at least from a woman.

He rose to his feet.

"I will bid you good-day, Miss Lingfield. I think we both should have time to consider where our conversation has led us. I shall take the opportunity of calling on you tomorrow or perhaps the next day when we can discuss your future more thoroughly."

"I assure you, that is quite unnecessary," Valeta answered. "If I think of anything I wish to say I will send you a note by hand."

"I find it easier to talk than to write," the Marquis replied, "so I shall call in person."

Knowing that his insistence annoyed her, he walked towards the door with a faint twinkle in his eyes.

When he reached it he looked back to see that she had not followed him.

"Good-bye, Miss Lingfield or, as that sounds rather formal, perhaps owing to our new relationship I should call you Valeta."

There was no mistaking the anger in Valeta's eyes and the manner in which her lips parted as if to refuse him the privilege.

But the Marquis had already gone, shutting the door behind him and there was only the sound of his footsteps crossing the hall.

As he swung himself up into his Phaeton which was waiting outside the Manor House and drove his horses with a remarkable expertise down the small drive and out onto the road which would lead him back to Troon, the Marquis was smiling.

As she heard the wheels of the Marquis's Phaeton drive away Valeta, her hands clenched, stood where he had left her, aware that she was trembling with fury.

"How dare he treat me in such a cavalier fashion?" she said. "How could Papa have made him my Guardian?"

She knew that the only thing she wanted at the moment was to be sure that never again would she set eyes on the Marquis, never again listen to his drawling voice which seemed somehow indifferent to any insult she might hurl at him.

She had felt when he rose to say good-bye an insane impulse to strike him, perhaps to scratch his face, to behave in a manner which she knew would have horrified both her father and mother and indeed herself.

But never in her life, she told herself, had she met a man she hated more.

Everything she had heard about the Marquis had made her despise him, except of course, for his record in the war.

When her father had spoken of his gallantry and his courage she had felt a respect for the young man whose father had shown her family quite a considerable amount of kindness.

The old Marquis had been an autocrat who thought that few people deserved his interest and who could count his personal friends on the fingers of one hand.

Yet because he had liked Sir Charles Lingfield, he had often asked him to shoot and once or twice a year he and his wife had dined at the great house.

When the old Marquis had died Sir Charles had in fact, been genuinely sad at losing him, but when the new Marquis had left his Regiment the whole atmosphere at Troon had altered over night.

The parties he gave in London and in the country lost nothing in the telling.

The servants in both houses in the majority

came from the estate and their relatives were regaled with stories which Valeta knew made the older folk feel as if their hair was standing on end.

Her father tried to find excuses for the new Marquis.

"It is the reaction from war," he said. "After all, he has been abroad fighting for a number of years and that takes its toll of every man."

"You do not behave in such an outrageous way, Papa," Valeta said.

Her father had smiled.

"I am too old and I cannot afford it."

"I do not believe, even if you could, you would ever do such things," Valeta said, "and the Marquis's money could be better spent in many other ways."

"Give him a chance," her father had pleaded good-humouredly. "He has generations of ancestors behind him who served their country in time of war and in time of peace."

It did not appear, Valeta thought, as if the young Marquis had any idea of serving anyone, except himself.

She heard of the presents he gave to the young women who graced the boards at Covent Garden and Drury Lane, and of the wild, daring exploits undertaken because he had been challenged to prove himself a better rider or finer pistol-shot than another man.

The whole estate learned of a Phaeton race from London to Newmarket which involved a collision between two of the competitors and resulted in three horses having to be shot.

"I have never heard before of a man of that age behaving in such a ridiculous fashion!" Valeta stormed.

Her father had sighed.

"He has certainly proved a disappointment so far," he agreed, "but I expect he will settle down sooner or later."

"The sooner the better!" Valeta had exclaimed. "It is time he took an interest in the estate. Andrews is too old to be the Agent and he does not like listening to stories of trouble or hardship."

"That is true," her father answered, "and it would be an excellent thing if the Marquis could only see for himself how much needs to be done here."

"Perhaps you could suggest it to him, Papa."

"You do not suppose I ever see the Marquis alone?" her father replied. "He is kind enough to ask me to his parties, but that is a very different thing."

"Very different," Valeta agreed.

When her father was brought back dead the morning after the Marquis's Steeple-Chase she thought that she would have rejoiced if she had learnt that he had broken his neck at the same time.

"I hate him! I hate him!" she said to herself now, "and somehow, some day, perhaps I will be able to get even with him."

Then she told herself it was the wishful thinking of a child.

The Marquis was impervious to anything she could do to him, and what was more, he was her Guardian.

Valeta walked slowly across the Drawing-Room and down the passage which led to the kitchen.

She found Nanny as she expected, sitting at the kitchen-table sewing.

Valeta had asked her over and over again to come and sit with her in the more comfortable rooms in the house, but Nanny was used to the kitchen and it was where she said she felt more comfortable.

She looked up now as Valeta entered and there was no mistaking the curiosity in her tired old eyes.

"Well?" she questioned.

Valeta sat down at the table before she answered. Then she said:

"I think, without exception, the Marquis is the wickedest man in the whole world!"

"How has he been upsetting you?" Nanny asked sharply. "Surely he only came to make his apologies which he should have made before now?"

"There is more to it than that."

"What do you mean?" Nanny asked.

"I cannot believe it is true," Valeta replied with a desperate note in her voice, "but Papa made him my Guardian!"

Nanny put down her sewing.

"Is that true?" she asked.

Valeta nodded.

There was silence while the old woman began to fold up the nightgown she had been mending.

"Well," she said at length, "you might do worse. You certainly need a Guardian in the position you're in now, and the Marquis is a very rich man."

Valeta gasped.

"What are you saying, Nanny? Can you not see that is the most terrible thing that could have happened?"

"I'm not so sure," Nanny answered. "It was worrying me what you would do with yourself with no money and nothing to look forward to. Well, if the Marquis does his duty, we should see a lot of changes in the future."

Valeta started to her feet.

"You are as bad as he is! My future is here with you, and not all the Marquises in the world are going to make me do anything different!"

"I shouldn't be too sure of that," Nanny replied. "After all, a Guardian's in the same position as a parent and His Lordship will have the right to say what you can and can't do."

"Nanny, what has come over you?" Valeta cried. "You sound as if you are pleased! How can you want this monster, this man who is responsible for Papa's death, to order me about and tell me what I am to do?"

"We'll wait and see, dearie," Nanny answered, "but it strikes me there might be some advantage in this for you, one way or another. Yes, we'll wait and see!"

CHAPTER THREE

"I consider," the Marquis said in an authoritative voice, "that you should have told me before now of the situation on the Estate."

"It has not been easy to have a private conversation with Your Lordship," the Agent replied, and added: "I wish, M'Lord, to resign my position. I've now served your esteemed father and Your Lordship for thirty-two years and it is time for me to retire."

The Marquis was silent for a moment. Then he said:

"If that is what you wish to do, Andrews, of course I understand, and I can only thank you most sincerely for all you have done for the Estate during those years."

The Agent bowed his head in acknowledgement of the compliment. Then he said hesitatingly:

"It's just a question, M'Lord —"

"You may choose a house that suits you," the Marquis interposed, before he could say any more, "or alternatively, accept a lump sum in lieu of accommodation, should you wish to live elsewhere."

"I was thinking, M'Lord, of returning to my own County which is Somerset, where I have an unmarried sister."

"In which case I am sure you will find that the

pension to which you will be entitled and the capital sum which I have just offered will enable you to live in comfort to the end of your days."

"I thank Your Lordship."

The Marquis rose and the two men shook hands. Then the Agent walked from the room, closing the Library door quietly behind him.

The Marquis threw himself back in his chair and was staring into space when Freddie entered.

"I saw your visitor leave," he said. "What about that ride we planned?"

"He was not a visitor," the Marquis answered, "but my Agent, or rather, my ex-Agent, as he has just handed me his resignation."

"Does that worry you?" Freddie asked. "He looked to me a bit old for the job."

"He is," the Marquis answered, "and as I have just discovered, somewhat out-of-date in his methods. But that does not make it any easier for me to find a successor."

"You have no-one in mind?" Freddie asked.

"No-one, unless you think Lionel would be suitable for the job!" the Marquis replied.

"I have a suggestion to make," Freddie said ignoring the sarcasm in the Marquis's tone, "but I do not like to interfere."

"You are not interfering," the Marquis answered. "It is all that damned girl's fault! Since she needled me into looking into things, I find I am beset by problems, the chief of which is to find myself a new Agent."

"That is where I can help you," Freddie said, "and incidentally, 'that damned girl', as you call her, has done you a good turn."

"What do you mean by that?"

"I mean that it is about time you started to take an interest in your possessions, and I do not mean the pictures on the walls, or the wine that your guests imbibe so freely."

"I know what you mean," the Marquis said in a disagreeable voice, "but there is a hell of a lot to do and it is going to take up a great deal of my time."

Freddie started to make the obvious retort, then bit back the words.

"You were about to make a suggestion as to a new Agent," the Marquis observed. "You know of one?"

"A very efficient one, as it happens."

"For God's sake tell me about him."

"That is exactly what I am trying to do. He is the son of my father's Agent, and has been working with him for the last five years since he stopped a bullet in his leg and was invalided out of the Army."

"This is no place for cripples."

"He is not that, only it took him over a year to recover and so he stayed at home, learning under his father. He is an excellent man in every way."

"And you think he would come to me?"

"I am sure of it. My father was only saying last time I was home that he thought it was time John Stevens had a job of his own."

"I would certainly like to see him."

"I will send a letter off to my father immediately," Freddie said, "asking him to tell Stevens to come here with all speed. That at least will solve one of your problems."

"If I engage him," the Marquis conceded.

"Of course! The decision rests with Your Supreme Highness!" Freddie laughed mockingly.

"Shut up, Freddie!" the Marquis retorted. "You know it is important that I should like the man if I am to work with him."

"I am delighted to hear that you intend to supervise your land personally," Freddie said. "If you ask me, you will find it very interesting. I know my father says that he never has a dull moment and very few free ones."

The Marquis laughed.

"That is just what I am afraid of. What will the dressing-rooms of Drury Lane do without me? And I have a feeling that quite a number of 'Incomparables' will go into mourning."

"The trouble with you," Freddie said, "is that you are too puffed up with your own conceit. I suppose you have never asked yourself how many women would be left clinging round your neck despite your looks, if you had no title and no money."

"Fortunately that is a situation which is unlikely to arise," the Marquis replied, "so there is no point in speculating about it."

"I know it is a question I would ask myself,

especially if I was getting married," Freddie said.

The Marquis shot him a quick glance.

"Still harping on about Dilys?"

"I had a letter from her this morning."

"You had a letter from Dilys?" the Marquis asked incredulously. "What about?"

"She wanted me to tell her confidentially what you were up to and why you had not gone back to London, as she understood you had intended to do."

"She asked you to spy on me?"

"I suppose you could put it that way."

"I know Dilys's methods only too well," the Marquis said. "You can tell her I am extremely occupied with the first love of my life, which happens to be Troon."

"She will be extremely suspicious of that piece of information," Freddie said, "and, although I know it is the truth, I doubt if she will believe me."

"It really does not matter whether she believes you or not!"

Freddie raised his eye-brows and the Marquis added:

"I have decided not to get married, at least for the moment. And what is more, I am too busy! Come on, let us go riding."

The Marquis walked ahead and he therefore did not see that Freddie's eyes were twinkling as he followed him.

They rode for nearly two hours, and when they turned for home their horses were moving more slowly and it was therefore possible to talk.

To Freddie's surprise the Marquis was obviously thinking deeply about his land and the way it was being farmed.

"I was just wondering," he said aloud, "whether we are using the most up-to-date methods possible. Who do you think would be in a position to show me what is being done in other parts of the country?"

"I believe Coke in Leicester knows more about agriculture than any other man in England. At least I have heard my father say so," Freddie replied.

"Then I shall make a point of visiting him," the Marquis said. "I feel sure we could improve our crops, although this year certainly looks promising."

Freddie was surprised, but he knew that when the Marquis really concentrated on a subject he considered it in all its aspects.

He thought to himself that 'that damned girl' had certainly started a new train of thought which might lead anywhere.

As they reached the great house which looked magnificent with the afternoon sunshine glinting on its hundreds of windows Freddie said:

"Do you mind if I go to the stables? I want to have a word with your Head Groom. One of the horses which I drove here seemed a bit off colour."

"Then Archer will soon tell you what is wrong," the Marquis replied. "But do not be too long. I thought we might have a game of tennis before dinner."

"A good idea!" Freddie answered.

Part of the out-buildings comprised a Royal tennis court where the ball game that had been popular since the reign of Henry VII was played and at which the Marquis excelled.

As it happened, he and Freddie were about equal performers and they found it an excellent way of taking exercise of which neither of them ever seemed to have enough.

A groom was waiting at the front door and the Marquis swung himself from the saddle, patted his horse's neck and walked up the steps into the Great Hall.

To his astonishment there appeared to be no footmen on duty, and he could hear raised voices coming from the Salon.

Putting his hat down on a chair, he walked across the marble floor, a frown between his eyes, as he wondered what could be causing such a noise and why the front door was left unattended.

He entered the open door of the Salon to see with astonishment that his Butler and footmen were all halfway down the room with their backs to him, having apparently an altercation with a large, extremely dirty red-faced man who was shouting abuse at both of them and at a slim figure standing in front of the mantelpiece.

It was impossible amid the turmoil to distinguish exactly what was being said, but the Marquis knew by a defiant attitude which he recognised that the latter was obviously the cause of contention.

For a moment he was stunned into silence by both the noise and the fact that such an altercation was taking place under his own roof.

Then as the voices seemed to grow louder he asked in a tone that cut like a whip through the confusion:

"What the devil is going on here?"

The Butler and the footmen turned hastily towards him looking guilty, but the big dirty man facing Valeta did not seem to hear.

"Oi tell ye ter hand 'im over!" he shouted, "or Oi'll get th' law t' tell ye 'e's mine."

"I will not let you ill-treat him any further!"

Even though Valeta spoke without raising her voice the Marquis could hear the anger beneath the surface as he walked towards her.

The footmen moved back hastily as the Marquis passed them and now the large dirty man realised something untowards was happening and turned his head.

"Who are you?" the Marquis asked, "and what are you doing in this room?"

Realising to whom he was speaking, the man was immediately obsequious.

"Oi be Cibber, the Sweep, M'Lord," he said, "an' engaged ter clean Yer Lordship's chimleys."

The Marquis looked towards Valeta.

"What is the trouble here?" he asked, "and

why should it concern you?"

"It should concern anyone with any decency in them," Valeta replied. "Look at this child and see the way he has been treated!"

She stepped to one side as she spoke and the Marquis saw cowering behind her a small boy, black with soot except where his tears had washed rivulets down his thin face.

" 'E belong ter me," the Sweep averred before the Marquis could speak, "an' bein' foolish and none too good at 'is job, 'e's come down th' wrong chimley. Oi'll take 'im away, M'Lord, this moment an' teach 'im not to do it again."

"You will do nothing of the sort!" Valeta retorted. "The boy is ill, besides being abominably scared."

She turned her face to the Marquis saying:

"Look at the child's elbows. They are raw and bleeding, and so are his knees. I heard this man with my own ears threaten to thrash him to within an inch of his life for coming down the wrong chimney."

" 'Twere just a matter o' speech, M'Lord," the Sweep said quickly. " 'E's a stupid boy, an' if Oi sometimes give 'im th' rough edge o' me tongue it don't do 'im no 'arm."

"He — burned my — feet!" the child whimpered.

"I am sure he did," Valeta said, "and that is something he shall never do again."

" 'E lies!" the Sweep said. " 'E lies an' lies! Ye can't believe a word 'e says."

72

"I believe him, seeing the condition he is in," Valeta said. "I would not allow an animal to be treated as this little boy has been."

" 'E's mine, an' ye've no roight ter interfere!" the Sweep shouted.

It was obvious that his anger, which had been dampened down by the Marquis's appearance, was now rising again.

"That will be quite enough!" the Marquis said sharply. "You will be quiet and not speak in that manner to a lady in my presence. Is that clear?"

"Yus, M'Lord. O' course, M'Lord. Oi'll do wot ye say, M'Lord," the Sweep said. "But th' boy be mine an' nobody ain't got no roight to int'fere in 'is apprenticeship, 'as Y'Lordship well knows."

"You will wait outside," the Marquis said firmly, "while I discuss this matter. Andrews!"

The footmen had all disappeared from the Salon where they had no right to be in the first place, but the Butler had remained standing by the door.

"Yes, M'Lord?"

"Take this man outside and put him somewhere where he can wait while I discuss the matter of this climbing boy with Miss Lingfield."

"Very good, M'Lord."

The Butler with a disdainful expression on his face, beckoned to the Sweep.

"Come this way, my man," he said, "and be careful how you do so."

The Sweep looked at the Marquis as if he was

about to challenge the order, but the expression on His Lordship's face made him know that he would be wise to keep his mouth shut.

He gave however, one furious glance at Valeta before he followed the Butler from the Salon and the door shut behind them.

"Now," the Marquis said, "perhaps you will explain what you are doing here, and what you expect me to do about that extremely dirty boy who is not improving the rug on which he is sitting."

"The rug can be cleaned," Valeta replied, looking down at the soot which had fallen from the boy's clothes.

As if she felt the Marquis had some right to demand an explanation she went on more quietly:

"I came here to see my father's Will, as you suggested I could do. I was waiting for them to find your Comptroller when this wretched child came tumbling down the chimney. He was crying and as you can see for yourself his elbows and knees are bleeding."

She paused for a moment before she went on:

"Before I could ask him any questions the door burst open and that monstrous man came in threatening to thrash him within an inch of his life, as obviously he has done on many occasions before, for making a mistake. The child is terrified of him, and not surprisingly."

"He burned my feet!" the boy whimpered again. "He lights a fire underneath me so that I have to go up and up."

The memory of what he had suffered brought fresh tears and Valeta sat down beside him and taking her handkerchief gave it into his grimy hand.

"Do not cry," she said. "I promise you shall not go back to him."

The Marquis saw that her white gown was getting marks of soot on it from her contact with the small boy but it did not seem to trouble her.

There was a softness in her voice which was something he had never heard before.

"Come over here," the Marquis said. "I want to speak to you."

He walked as he spoke away from the hearthrug towards the window and after a moment's pause Valeta rose to follow him. He saw her touch the boy's head with a consoling gesture before she left him.

When she reached the Marquis's side she looked down with an expression of consternation at the soot on her hands.

With a faint smile he took a clean linen handkerchief from the pocket of his riding-coat and handed it to her.

"You cannot touch pitch," he said, "without being defiled."

He saw her eyes flash because she thought he was laughing at her, but she took the handkerchief and wiped her hands.

"He cannot go back to that man," she said as though nothing was of consequence except the child.

"You must be aware that an apprentice belongs to his Master," the Marquis said.

"Have you any idea how these children suffer?" Valeta asked.

She spoke in a low voice so that the boy could not overhear and the Marquis saw by the expression in her eyes how moved she was by his plight.

"Chimneys have to be swept," he replied.

"Have you read the findings of the Select Committee who were appointed to look into the plight of climbing boys?"

There was a moment's silence before the Marquis replied:

"As a matter of fact I have not, but I have heard there have been protests made against their employment."

"Then perhaps you are unaware," Valeta said, "that the official minimum age of these boys is supposed to be eight, but children of four to six are often forced up the chimneys."

The Marquis did not reply and she went on:

"They have to climb up half-blind and choked by soot, and either an older boy is sent up behind them to jab a pin into their bare foot to keep them going or they are driven up by the Master Sweep lighting hay or straw beneath them, as this fiend was doing."

"I will speak to the man about his methods," the Marquis said, "but, as I have already said, an apprentice belongs to his master."

"Not if he is a brute and practically a murderer!" Valeta flashed.

She stared at the Marquis disdainfully as she went on:

"The Society which has demanded the abolition of climbing boys has pointed out that there are alternative methods of cleaning and sweeping chimneys, but I suppose Your Lordship is not interested."

Now there was no disguising the contempt in her voice and the hatred in her eyes, and after a moment the Marquis said:

"Perhaps I had better send for Chamberlain and see what he can do in this matter."

"I should have thought it was a problem you could cope with yourself, if you wished to do so," Valeta retorted.

"What do you suggest I do?" the Marquis asked.

For a moment he thought she had no answer. Then she replied:

"Surely it would be possible to buy the child's freedom?"

The Marquis did not reply and she said:

"Perhaps it might cost the same as a brooch or a bracelet you would give to your lady-friends in London, or even as much as one of your much publicised parties, but at least you would have the satisfaction of knowing that you had saved a small child from a living hell."

The Marquis knew by the way she spoke that she doubted if he would do such a thing, and he had an impulse to tell her that she was quite right in her opinion of him and that he would not stir a finger to help the boy.

Then he heard the child whimper and knew that much as he was reluctant to interfere Valeta was right and he could not give him back to his Master.

"You had better leave this to me," he said abruptly, and turning walked from the room.

Valeta gave a deep sigh as if some of the tension with which she had fought the Marquis went out of her.

Then she went back to the hearth-rug and knelt down beside the little boy.

When the Marquis came back into the room he found that Valeta had somehow managed to clean the boy's face of soot and he was no longer crying.

He realised that the blackened rag she held in her hand was what was left of his superfine linen handkerchief.

There was a cynical smile on his face as he looked down into Valeta's questioning eyes.

"You were quite right," he said. "The cost was the equivalent of a diamond bracelet."

"You . . . bought him?"

He could hardly hear the words.

"I bought his apprenticeship," he replied. "He is the first present that your Guardian has been able to give you. I only hope he does not prove to be too troublesome."

"You have bought him!" Valeta exclaimed. "Oh, thank you! Thank you!"

She rose to her feet and her eyes seemed to

hold the sunshine in them.

"That was kind, very kind. You are quite certain that cruel man will not be able to demand him back?"

"If he tries let me know," the Marquis answered, "for I now have it in writing that Nicholas — that apparently is the boy's name — is no longer his apprentice."

"I am grateful. Deeply grateful!" Valeta said. "Now I had better take him home."

"You have some mode of conveyance?" the Marquis enquired.

"A pony-cart."

"I will order it round from the stables, but first I think it would be wise to ask one of the servants to clean your new protegé up a little. He has obviously ruined part of my house, there is no reason why he should do the same to yours."

Valeta's lips twitched as she looked down at the mess on the rug.

"He is very dirty," she said, "and when I give him a bath it is going to make his wounds smart painfully."

"I only hope he appreciated the trouble you are taking over him," the Marquis said dryly.

Valeta was not listening, as she looked at the boy speculatively. Then she said:

"Perhaps if your Housekeeper can give me an old sheet we could bundle him up in it so that he would not make too much mess until I get him home."

"I am sure that can be arranged," the Marquis

said. "You are quite certain you would not like my housemaids to clean him up a little?"

"Nanny and I will manage," Valeta replied. "Thank you very much for being so kind."

It was doubtful if the Marquis heard the end of her sentence for he had gone to the door and was telling Andrews to fetch a sheet as Valeta had suggested.

As the small boy sat on the hearth-rug looking at them apprehensively with wide eyes, the Marquis drew Valeta aside again to say:

"We will have to find foster-parents for this boy."

"I think the first thing is to feed him," Valeta answered. "You can see he is little more than skin and bone, and I have the feeling, although I may be wrong, that he is well-bred."

She paused before she said:

"He may even be one of the children who have been stolen from a decent home as was described in the report of the Select Committee."

She knew as she spoke that the Marquis was thinking she was making a fairy-tale out of it, but he merely said:

"I hope you are right, and I hope too, he will not prove so obstreperous that he wrecks your house before we can find more suitable accommodation for him."

The Housekeeper appeared with a large linen sheet and a surprised expression on her face.

When she saw the mess the boy had made on the hearth-rug she held up her hands in horror.

"It'll take me a long time to get that rug clean, M'Lord," she said, "and I've thought for some time we should get a better Sweep than that man Cibber. If you ask me, he doesn't know his job."

"This is your opportunity," Valeta said to the Marquis in a low voice, "to employ a Sweep who does not use wretched children to clean the chimneys."

"I had heard there are various alternative methods," the Marquis said, "before you mentioned it, but I have always been told they are not very effective."

He saw by the expression on Valeta's face that he had aroused her anger again, but before she could answer him he said:

"I promise you, however, that I will look into it."

"Thank you, My Lord," she said. "Unless you are a sadist I cannot help believing you will at least give a trial to another method."

"I am told," the Marquis said merely to tease her, "that in Ireland geese are sometimes drawn up chimneys."

"That too is disgustingly cruel!" Valeta exclaimed. "But perhaps Your Lordship and I can discuss it another time."

"I will call on you tomorrow," the Marquis answered, but Valeta did not seem to have heard him.

She had turned to the small boy and was drawing him very gently to his feet from the position into which he had collapsed when he had first come down the chimney.

She could hear the Housekeeper behind her making tut-tutting noises of disapproval as she looked at the amount of soot there was in the fireplace and on the rug.

Valeta said nothing, but merely went on wrapping the boy in the clean sheet before she said to him:

"Now, Nicholas, we are going for a drive behind my pony. You will enjoy that."

"You'll not give me back to Mr. Cibber?" the child whimpered.

It was obvious from the alarm in his voice that he was terrified of the man.

"No, no, you belong to me now," Valeta said. "That horrid man shall never hurt you again — I promise you!"

"You are sure? — quite sure?"

It struck the Marquis listening that the boy spoke in an unusually refined manner for a child from the back streets.

Perhaps Valeta was right and he was better bred than he appeared to be, covered as he was in soot and with his eyes swollen from crying.

She had wrapped the small child up like a cocoon in the big sheet but now Valeta wondered a little helplessly how she would get him out of the house.

It would be best, she decided, if she carried him and bent forward to pick him up when the Marquis said:

"Wait. I will send for your pony-cart and get

one of the footmen to carry the boy."

"That's right. M'Lord," the Housekeeper approved. "He'll drop more soot on the rest of the carpet if he moves from there. I've never seen such a mess!"

"I am sure you will be able to clean it away," Valeta said, "and I think too you are right. That horrible man, Cibber, is a very inexperienced Sweep. There must be someone better you can employ."

"It's the rag-tag and bobtail in the sweep business nowadays, Miss," the Housekeeper replied. "Before the war the chimney sweeps were all skilled men, but now I'm told farm labourers have gone into the business hoping to earn more money."

"I am sure that is true," Valeta replied, "and boys are sold to them by their parents for three or four guineas."

"Is that a fact, Miss?" the Housekeeper asked. "Then it's a scandal! That's what it is!"

"I agree with you," Valeta said. "And in the report I read it said that a lot of the boys had even been kidnapped!"

"The Government should do something about it," the Housekeeper declared.

"Of course they should," Valeta agreed looking at the Marquis meaningfully as she spoke.

She thought she saw a cynical smile on his lips and hated him more than she did already.

"Little boys like this," she said to the Housekeeper, "are often given no food except what they can steal. They have to sleep on the floor and never get the chance of being washed, and their masters treat them with appalling cruelty!"

She was trying to speak calmly because she wished to make the Housekeeper agree that the climbing boys should no longer be used at Troon, but she could not help her voice breaking and the tears coming into her eyes.

Almost as if he was embarrassed the Marquis said:

"I think your pony-cart will be round by now, and here is James to carry your new acquisition."

A tall, stalwart young footman resplendent in his livery walked towards them as the Marquis spoke.

"Be very careful!" Valeta warned as he reached the child wrapped in the sheet. "He has been badly hurt."

The footman picked the boy up gingerly and although Valeta saw Nicholas wince he did not cry out.

They walked in a strange procession, the footman going first followed by Valeta, the Housekeeper, and lastly the Marquis.

The pony-cart drawn by one old pony which Valeta used to ride before she grew too big for it was waiting at the bottom of the steps.

Nicholas was placed carefully on the seat and Valeta picked up the reins.

"Thank you very much, My Lord," she said to the Marquis.

He inclined his head but did not speak as she drove off.

Only as she was going down the drive did he realise that Mrs. Fielding his Housekeeper was still standing beside him watching her go.

"That is a very determined young woman, Mrs. Fielding!" he said aloud.

"And a very kind-hearted one, M'Lord."

"Kind-hearted?" the Marquis queried, thinking that was the last description he, personally would have applied to Valeta.

"Yes, indeed, M'Lord. It's wonderful the way she's taken over her mother's good works in looking after the people in the village."

"Looking after them?" the Marquis enquired. "Why should they need looking after?"

Mrs. Fielding looked at him in surprise.

"Surely Your Lordship is aware that the Vicar has no wife? I'm told he often says he wouldn't know what he'd do without Miss Valeta helping him in visiting the sick, getting the children to Sunday-School, and a dozen other things for which a Clergyman depends upon his wife."

"Miss Lingfield seems very young for that sort of work."

"It's no a question of age, M'Lord, it's a question of heart, and when one has a big heart there's always others as benefits."

The Marquis said nothing, he merely walked back into the house.

The following afternoon Valeta was not surprised as she looked out of the window to see the Marquis's Phaeton coming down their small drive.

Her eyes lingered with appreciation on the magnificent horses which drew it, and although she hated him, she could not help realising that the Marquis was an intrinsic part of his ultra-smart turn out.

With his high-crowned hat at an angle on his dark head, his grey whip-cord coat fitting him like a glove, and his champagne-coloured pantaloons above his shining Hessians he was a picture of Fashion.

Yet at the same time he was so essentially masculine that his clothes were a part of him in a way which had been recommended by Beau Brummel.

Because she wished to be formal Valeta hurried into the Drawing-Room, seated herself by the empty fireplace, waiting until Nanny announced the Marquis:

"The Marquis of Troon, Miss Valeta!"

Without hurrying, Valeta rose to her feet slowly and gracefully telling herself it was absurd to feel her heart beating a little more quickly and that she was surprisingly nervous.

Ever since the Marquis's first visit she had sworn that she would not be intimidated by him, and she would never, in any circumstances be afraid of him.

And yet she knew because he was in himself, such an essentially positive person, she had the feeling that he overwhelmed her and she must fight desperately to preserve her own individuality.

He reached her and she curtseyed.

"Good-afternoon, My Lord!"

"Good-afternoon, Valeta."

She felt his use of her Christian name was an impertinence, but it was unimportant beside so much else that concerned her at the moment and she was not prepared to make an issue of it.

"May I sit down?" the Marquis asked.

"Of course," Valeta replied. "May I offer Your Lordship some refreshment?"

"No, thank you," he answered. "I wish of course, to know how your protegé is."

Her eyes lit up.

"I was right! I was absolutely right! He *is* well-bred and I am certain he was stolen from his parents."

"How can you be sure of that?"

Valeta seated herself opposite the Marquis and bent forward eagerly.

"First because he obviously found it quite natural to have a bath."

She gave a little smile as she added:

"Your Lordship will not know, but I can assure you that, if ever it has been necessary to bathe one of the village children, they have shrieked in horror at such an imposition. But Nicholas not only enjoyed his bath, but at the end of it he said: 'I feel clean'!"

"And have you done that?"

"We removed a great deal of the soot, but it is

ingrained into the skin, and will obviously take time. I gather that his only bed has been sacks of soot in a damp cellar where that fiend kept his boys."

"Are there many of them?"

"Three others, but they are much older than Nicholas."

"What else did you discover about him?" the Marquis asked.

He found himself surprisingly interested.

He had thought when he was driving to the Manor that doubtless by this time Valeta would be disillusioned by her new toy, finding him as rough and foul-mouthed as were most of the boys who came from the slums of London.

He would not have been surprised if Valeta had pleaded with him to take the boy away immediately, saying that neither she nor her old Nurse could cope with him.

"He was cruelly beaten," Valeta was saying in a low voice. "There are weals from a whip on his back and on his legs, and because he has cried the soot has got into his eyes and they are still red and swollen."

She drew in her breath before she continued:

"But his features are refined and already he is beginning to forget the rough words he has learned from the other boys and to talk in the same way that I do, which I am quite certain is natural to him."

"How old do you think he is?" the Marquis asked.

"Six at the most. I have not questioned him yet about where he comes from, but when we gave him food to eat, he handled his knife and fork as any gentleman's son might do."

Her voice was excited as she added:

"This is important, he looked at a silver spoon and said: 'My Dadda had one like this'."

Valeta waited for the Marquis's reaction to her story.

"I am very interested in what you are telling me," he said. "Personally, I have always disbelieved stories of children being kidnapped, but I expect you are going to ask me to make enquiries from the Police, and I will do so, if that is what you wish."

"That is certainly one of the things I was going to ask you to do," Valeta replied. "I suppose the Police will help, although I believe they are shockingly under-manned."

"How do you know that?" the Marquis asked in surprise. But he was aware that she was speaking the truth.

Those who lived in London had been concerned about the lack of organisation of the Police and their hopelessly inadequate pay.

This inevitably resulted in too many of them being dishonest.

It was one thing, the Marquis thought, for him to know such matters, but how could Valeta, living in the country, be aware of what was happening in London?

She had, however, an answer to his question

which he did not expect.

"I read a newspaper every day, My Lord," she replied, "and also my father and I studied reports of the last two enquiries that were published by the Select Committee of the House of Commons."

The Marquis was astonished.

Only a few men with whom he associated in the Social World took the trouble to read the findings of the Select Committees, and no woman of his acquaintance had even heard of such a thing.

As if she felt she ought to explain a little further Valeta said:

"My mother's father was the Bishop of London, and my mother was always deeply interested in the work that he and his clergy did to try to relieve some of the terrible suffering amongst the poor in the City."

"I had no idea," the Marquis murmured.

"Papa became interested too, and so I grew up realising that those who were fortunate to be born into a happy home, as I was, must try to help others in very different circumstances."

The way she spoke told the Marquis that she was utterly and completely sincere.

Yet as he listened to her he thought how lovely she would look if her hair was dressed in a fashionable style and there was a necklace of jewels round her throat and her gown had been made by a skilful dressmaker.

"Such beauty is wasted," he told himself, "on

worrying over climbing boys, dishonest policemen and doubtless innumerable other vices and horrors that are the inevitable result of poverty."

"I think, Valeta," he said after a moment, "that while we are deeply concerned with the problem of Nicholas and his life, we have also to consider the problem of you!"

CHAPTER FOUR

"Do not worry about me now," Valeta said quickly, "I want to talk to you about Nicholas."

The Marquis raised his eye-brows.

It was unusual for any woman of his acquaintance not to be interested in herself, but he was listening as Valeta continued:

"I have been thinking about the best way to get in touch with Nicholas's parents, and while I am sure they would have notified their local Police, if they had any, and the Magistrates, their loss may not have percolated to London."

"I follow your line of thought," the Marquis said, "but what else can we do?"

There was a little pause and Valeta looked embarrassed.

"It might be . . . expensive," she said after a moment, hesitatingly, "but might not the best thing be to . . . advertise?"

The Marquis considered the idea for a moment, then he said:

"I am sure you are right. The difficulty of course is that we must cover a very wide field."

"That is why I was . . . afraid it might cost a lot of . . . money, but I would like to pay some of it myself."

The Marquis smiled.

"That is something I should certainly not allow you to do. Even if we have to advertise in every newspaper in England, I do not think it will bankrupt me!"

He saw the gratitude in Valeta's eye, without her having to say the words, and he went on:

"I can see that the problem of Nicholas means a great deal to you, and I only hope you will not be too disappointed if your efforts to find his parents fail."

Valeta clasped her hands together as she said in a low voice:

"You will think it very foolish of me, but I have the unmistakable feeling that we shall find that somehow it was meant that he should come down the chimney at the precise moment when I had come to your house to see your Comptroller."

"I am afraid Mrs. Fielding will not agree that it was a destined occasion," the Marquis said dryly. "She informed me this morning that she believes the hearth-rug is irretrievably ruined."

"I am sure she is wrong," Valeta said quickly. "Let me try to clean it. I am very good at that sort of thing."

"That 'sort of thing', as you call it," the Marquis said, "is not an occupation that befits my Ward."

He thought that Valeta might be abashed at his rebuke. Instead she burst out laughing.

"Are you really thinking of me in that capacity?" she asked. "What do you consider I should do? Sit on a silken cushion all day giving orders to a lot of nonexistent servants?"

The Marquis did not smile.

"I have been thinking about your future," he

said, "and I am more than ever convinced that you cannot stay here alone, with or without Nicholas as a protector."

"You would not wish me to . . . give him . . . up?" Valeta asked, afraid of the sarcasm in his voice.

"Supposing his parents do not turn up? You cannot expect to keep him for ever."

To the Marquis's surprise Valeta did not answer him, but rose to her feet to walk a little way from him towards the window.

"What are you thinking about?" he asked.

"I am thinking about Nicholas, and all the children like him who are suffering from intolerable cruelty which no-one does anything to prevent."

The little throb in Valeta's voice was inescapable and after a moment the Marquis said:

"You obviously do not know that the Chairman of the Select Committee who was appointed this year, Henry Grey Bennett, is trying to get a Bill passed through Parliament which will prohibit the use of small boys being used in the cleaning of chimneys."

"And you will support him?" Valeta asked eagerly.

The Marquis knew this was an important question to her, but he was not prepared to pledge himself to a course of action which he might not be able to keep.

"I am considering it," he said cautiously.

"Please . . . please," Valeta pleaded, "give it

your full support. I cannot bear to think of sensitive little boys like Nicholas being forced into such an . . . appalling trade."

Her voice broke before she added:

"I suppose you have heard that they usually become the victims of what is known as 'The Chimney-Sweepers' cancer'?"

The Marquis rose to his feet.

"Now listen to me, Valeta," he said, "I think you are letting Nicholas's plight prey on your mind. At your age you should be wishing to enjoy yourself, to go to Balls and meet people of your own position in life."

He saw by the expression on Valeta's face that she was not impressed by what he was saying, and he added more forcefully:

"You have saved Nicholas. Now let that be enough. You cannot prevent people from wanting to have their chimneys swept, or using what is the easiest method of doing so."

He saw that Valeta was going to argue once again about the alternatives to using climbing boys and went on, before she could speak:

"As I have become involved in looking after you I promise I will do the same for Nicholas. We will arrange some schooling for him and later, I am sure, there will be employment for him at Troon. But I am not taking on a whole army of climbing boys and that is final!"

He thought for a moment that Valeta was going to protest. Then she said:

"I am grateful . . . very grateful that you will

help Nicholas, and I do not want to be a . . . nuisance to you or bother you with my prejudices. It is just that I loathe cruelty and it seems intolerable in a rich country such as ours that there is so much suffering from extreme poverty about which no-one seems to care."

The Marquis ignored the plea in her voice and said:

"Now let us get back to you, because it is a subject which has to be discussed sooner or later."

"I am . . . sorry to be a . . . trouble."

She spoke humbly. Then as if some pride within herself resented it, she added in a different tone:

"I have already asked Your Lordship to forget about me. Everything is perfect as it is, as long as I can stay on here."

"I am not going back over that argument," the Marquis said firmly. "What I have decided to do is to take you tomorrow to call on my mother."

He saw the surprise in Valeta's eyes and knew it was also a surprise to him because the idea had not come to him until that very moment.

"Your mother?" Valeta repeated.

"She does not live in the Dower House, as might be expected, but about fifteen miles away in a house which my father bought for her because she found it so attractive. Some people find her a rather frightening person and she is very much a law unto herself, but I would like you to meet her and I am sure she will have ideas of what you can do in the future."

There was silence for a moment. Then Valeta asked:

"Do you really . . . insist on my . . . meeting your . . . mother? I would much rather try to think of . . . someone who could come and live here with me if you . . . insist on a Chaperon."

"You have someone in mind?" the Marquis asked.

Valeta hesitated.

"I had a Governess of whom I was very fond. I am afraid she is old and not in particularly good health, but I am sure she could be persuaded to come to me, at least for a long visit."

Valeta did not add that her Governess and her Nurse had never got on well together.

She would not for a moment have suggested that Miss Colgrave should come to her except that she was afraid of the Marquis's plans for her future, and she wished to be involved with him as little as possible.

The Marquis thought the idea of any young girl as lovely as Valeta being shut up with two old women, one in ill health, was a quite ridiculous proposition, but aloud he said:

"I think it would be wise to try my way first, and for you to meet my mother. If you do not like her suggestions, then of course we will consider the idea of inviting your Governess to be your guest."

"At what time would you like me to be ready?" Valeta asked.

"I will send a groom to my mother to say that we will have luncheon with her," the Marquis replied, "so I will call for you at about eleven o'clock."

"I will be ready," Valeta said, "and perhaps I ought to thank Your Lordship."

"There is no need," the Marquis replied. "I am getting used to your reluctance to acquiesce in my plans and your efforts to twist me round to your way of thinking. But perhaps one day you will be obliged to acknowledge I am right."

"I am very . . . grateful to Your Lordship about Nicholas."

"We were not talking about Nicholas," the Marquis replied. "Nevertheless I will tell Chamberlain to send out advertisements immediately to all the County newspapers, and we will also advertise in 'The Morning Post' and 'The Times'."

"Thank you . . . thank you!" Valeta cried.

This time there was no doubting her sincerity.

The Marquis took his watch from his waistcoat pocket and was just about to say he must leave when Valeta asked:

"Would you like to see Nicholas?"

The Marquis had the feeling as Valeta spoke that she expected him to refuse, and because she expected it, he answered:

"Most certainly! I was going to ask you to bring him to me. I have a feeling I shall find it hard to recognise him."

"I will fetch him at once!" Valeta said eagerly and hurried from the room.

The Marquis found himself smiling a little ruefully.

He had found himself in a great many unusual situations in his life, but never before, he thought, had he spent any time with a young woman who looked at him with an expression of hatred and whose only thought was for a climbing boy.

It was obvious, although it seemed incredible, that there had been no *Beaux* in Valeta's life and she had not the least idea of how to be flirtatious, or how to coax a man into doing what she wanted.

She had instead, the Marquis thought, gone at him bald-headed, and he had the uncomfortable feeling that if he saw much of her, he would find himself forced into the position of attending long and dreary debates in the House of Lords on Social Inequality, and even voting with the Radicals.

The idea made him frown because it brought him thoughts of Lionel.

Only that morning he had received a letter from one of his friends in London saying that Lionel had been seen making impassioned speeches in Trafalgar Square against the iniquities of wealthy landlords and employers who ground down those who worked for them.

The writer had finished:

"The name of Stevington had always been respected, and it is most unfortunate that your

brother should behave in this manner. I can only suggest that you remonstrate with him at the first opportunity."

The Marquis had thrown the letter down on the breakfast-table with a gesture of irritation.

He knew only too well that remonstrating with Lionel was a waste of time and always resulted in their both losing their tempers.

He was intelligent enough to understand that his brother's hatred of wealthy landlords was directed against himself and stemmed from jealousy and envy: he was not genuinely moved by the plight of the less fortunate members of society.

"What can I do about it?" the Marquis asked himself.

It made him think that Lionel with his sanctimonious and fundamentally insincere proselytising over the poor was bad enough, without having a Ward who had been thrust upon him by fate harping on more or less the same subject.

He was deciding that Valeta had definitely to be discouraged from becoming sentimental over such matters when the door opened and she came in leading Nicholas by the hand.

It would certainly have been impossible to recognise the soot-covered miserable child he had last seen sobbing on the hearth-rug in the good-looking, attractive little boy she led towards him.

Now that Nicholas's hair was washed it was fair, and his skin was pale.

As he looked at him, the Marquis realised that Valeta had been right in saying that his features were refined.

He was neatly dressed in clothes that were cheap and must have been purchased quickly from the village shop, but there was no doubt he carried himself in a manner which might easily be attributed to good breeding.

His hands, the Marquis noticed, had nothing coarse about them.

"Here is Nicholas!" Valeta said proudly to the Marquis, then added to the small boy: "This is the gentleman who saved you from that horrible Mr. Cibber. You must bow and thank him."

The Marquis was perceptive enough to notice that when Nicholas saw there was a man in the room, there had been a flicker of fear in his eyes.

Still holding tightly to Valeta's hand he bowed his head and said in a voice that shook a little:

"Thank you . . . for saving . . . me, Sir."

"I think it was really Miss Lingfield who did that," the Marquis said, "but you are safe now and so we must just forget everything that happened since you left your home."

Nicholas looked puzzled and the Marquis, to his own surprise, knelt down on one knee, so that he was face to face with the boy.

"Tell me about your home," he asked beguilingly. "Did your father have horses?"

For a moment it seemed as if the small boy did not understand the question. Then he said:

"I can ride. I have a pony."

"What is his name?" the Marquis asked quietly.

There was a pause, and it was obvious that Nicholas was thinking hard.

"Rufus!" he said at last. "My pony's name is Rufus!"

The Marquis straightened himself and looked at Valeta with a light of triumph in his eyes.

"That was clever of you," she said in a low voice. "I never thought of it, but of course at his age he would have ridden."

"It certainly gives us a clue as to his identity," the Marquis said. "Perhaps later he will describe to you the place he lived. It might save us from guessing whether it was the North, South, East or West of England!"

There was a sceptical note in his voice which Valeta thought she should resent.

Yet she was so grateful to him for being so pleasant to Nicholas that for a moment the hatred which flared every time she spoke to the Marquis seemed to have been dampened down.

"Now I must leave," the Marquis said. "I will call for you as we arranged at eleven o'clock to-morrow."

He was aware as soon as he spoke that Valeta was longing to dissuade him from doing anything of the sort, but without speaking she followed him, still holding Nicholas by the hand, across the small hall to the front door.

Outside the Marquis's Phaeton drawn by only two horses which he used when he was driving around the estate was waiting, the groom in his smart livery standing at the horses' heads.

Nicholas gave a little whoop of delight.

"A Phaeton!" he cried. "Like Dadda's."

He disengaged his hand from Valeta's and ran down the steps looking at the Phaeton, then at the horses with obvious delight.

"You see!" Valeta said breathlessly. "I was right!"

"We must certainly try to find his parents," the Marquis replied.

"He is a dear little boy," Valeta said, her eyes on Nicholas. "I have a feeling when we do find them, I shall be sorry to see him go."

"I think it would be more sensible for you to be thinking of getting married and having a family of your own," the Marquis remarked dryly.

Valeta did not reply but merely stiffened, and the Marquis stepped into his Phaeton and picked up the reins.

The groom stood back from the horses' heads and as they started to move off, he ran to swing himself agilely onto the seat behind.

Nicholas stood in the driveway watching, then clapped his hands together.

"A Phaeton!" he said almost to himself. "A Phaeton, like Dadda's!"

The Marquis had plenty to think about as he drove back through the Park towards Troon.

As he neared the great house he saw there was a carriage waiting outside the front door and before he saw the servants' livery or recognised the crest on the doors he knew to whom it belonged.

He had the uncomfortable feeling that he was in for a scene.

Without really meaning to, he drew in his horses so that they trotted a little slower as he descended the drive towards the bridge and crossing the lake moved towards the long flight of stone steps which led up to the front door.

He hoped that Freddie, who had gone trout-fishing, was back now, but when he entered the Hall the Butler said:

"Lady Dilys Powick has called, M'Lord, and is in the Blue Salon!"

"Is Captain Weyborne here?"

"No, M'Lord. Captain Weyborne has not yet returned."

The Marquis gave a little sigh and walked across the Hall to what was known as the Blue Salon.

It was a room that was habitually used for callers and the one into which Nicholas had descended from the chimney.

Lady Dilys was seated on a high-backed armchair which she was aware showed to advantage her auburn hair and sensationally white skin.

She had slightly slanting eyes which were accentuated by a touch of mascara at the corners and which gave her what her admirers described as a bewitching look.

As the Marquis entered the room now she smiled at him in a manner which was calculated to drive most men to madness, and certainly to make the blood run quicker in their veins.

The Marquis however, seemed quite unmoved as he walked towards her to say:

"I was not expecting you, Dilys. Why did you not send word that you were coming?"

"There is surely no need for that where we are concerned?" Lady Dilys replied in a low, seductive voice. "I was tired of waiting for you and wondering what you were doing here in the country."

"There are a great many things to occupy me," the Marquis answered, "the most immediate being that I have engaged a new Agent and have to instruct him in his duties."

Lady Dilys threw back her head and gave a silvery laugh.

"My dear Serle, how pompous that sounds! Since when have you concerned yourself with Agents and doubtless also with cattle and pigs? Be careful, or you may become bovine!"

"There is always that possibility," the Marquis said. "Have you really journeyed all this way from London to see me, or are you staying in the neighbourhood?"

"I am staying with you," Lady Dilys said sweetly. "A second carriage containing my luggage and my lady's-maid is following."

The Marquis frowned.

"I am not entertaining at the moment, with the exception of Freddie, and therefore you cannot stay here!"

"Am I really hearing you aright?" Lady Dilys asked. "Why should I not stay with you as we have often done in the past?"

"Not alone at Troon," the Marquis replied.

"But in a great number of other places."

"That is different!"

"Why?"

"Because Troon is my home, and I must keep up certain standards."

Again Lady Dilys laughed and it was not such a pretty sound.

"What has happened?" she asked. "What has come over you, Serle? I cannot believe that you are refusing to give me a roof over my head, if only for tonight."

"It may surprise you, Dilys, but I have no intention of allowing you to stay here when there is no other woman in the house."

Lady Dilys stared at him in astonishment before she cried:

"I think you are going mad! We have been together now for a long time, and never, never in the whole of our acquaintance have you ever fussed about the proprieties or talked about our having 'another woman' with us. As though that would make any difference to the manner in which we behaved!"

"What we do in private is one thing," the Marquis said, "in public another!"

Lady Dilys narrowed her eyes.

"You almost sound as if you were ashamed of me!"

"Not in the slightest," the Marquis replied, "but here at Troon I do not wish to cause a scandal or invite local gossip."

"And I suppose you think they did not gossip about the party you gave a month ago of which I was a member, or your Easter party which certainly would not have satisfied ecclesiastical standards?" Lady Dilys asked mockingly.

"I am prepared to admit that the two parties you mention were in themselves somewhat regrettable," the Marquis said, "but that is all the more reason not to add fuel to the fire by flouting the accepted conventions."

"If that is what you feel," Lady Dilys said softly, "then let us, by all means, behave in a manner of which everyone would approve by getting married!"

The Marquis told himself he might have expected that was what she would say and what she had intended when she came here, but somehow it was a blow to hear the actual words and to know that this was a trap that he must avoid with some dexterity.

It suddenly struck him that he had no desire whatsoever although he had once thought differently, to marry Lady Dilys.

He did not know why, but he felt as if he was suddenly free of her and she no longer had the power to move him either to admiration or desire.

Always in the past, her beauty which was undeniable, had made him feel it was a sheer delight to see her face and be lost in admiration at the perfection of her features: to be beguiled by her slanting eyes and curving red lips.

There had also been something about her which invariably quickened his pulses and made him want to touch her.

But now, inexplicably and so suddenly that he felt himself jolted by the truth of it, the allurement or whatever it had been, had gone.

She was beautiful, there was no denying that, but she might have been a picture or a cold marble statue for all the effect she now had on him physically.

And she was waiting, waiting for him to reply to what had been a proposal of marriage.

With an effort at a laugh that was unmistakably contrived the Marquis answered:

"That is certainly a rather strange suggestion, Dilys, for you know that neither you nor I are the marrying sort. If we were tied to each other for life, I am quite certain we would be bored with each other within a few weeks."

"That is not true, Serle. We are eminently suited to each other," Lady Dilys replied. "We think the same, we enjoy the same pleasures, however outrageous, and we enjoy — each other."

Her voice deepened on the last two words and there was a deliberate under-current in her tone which the Marquis did not miss.

Also she looked up at him as she spoke and he knew she was inviting him in a manner that she

108

believed was irresistible and which had always in the past, made him reach out to draw her into his arms.

But the Marquis did not move.

"I can only repeat, Dilys," he said, "that marriage with anyone would be my idea of unmitigated boredom!"

"If that is true," Lady Dilys said, "how delighted your brother Lionel will be!"

"Lionel?" the Marquis asked quickly, "what do you know about Lionel?"

"Ponsonby was telling me about the speeches he has been making against you. I am told there is a cartoon of him denouncing wealthy landlords like yourself, and inciting the rag-tag and bobtail with whom he associates, to burn down Carlton House."

There was a frown between the Marquis's eyes.

He knew how scurrilous cartoonists could be, but he had never thought any member of his family would figure in one.

"So you see, dearest Serle," Lady Dilys said, "the sooner you marry and produce an heir, the better!"

"There is still plenty of time for that," the Marquis said, "and not even to circumvent Lionel will I be forced up the aisle."

There was silence for a moment, and he knew that Lady Dilys was calculating her next move.

"If marriage does not concern us," the Marquis said briskly, "somewhere for you to stay the night does. I will send a note to Lady Forsett, asking her if she will put you up for the night. You will be quite comfortable and you will doubtless want to return to London tomorrow morning."

Lady Dilys rose gracefully from the chair in which she had been sitting.

As she did so, the ostrich feathers on her high-brimmed bonnet fluttered and the Marquis was conscious of the exotic fragrance which emanated from her.

It was a scent that was peculiarly her own and which all her lovers recognised as a haunting perfume which, the moment they smelt it, brought back irresistible memories of fire and passion.

The Marquis was forewarned of her intentions but he would not run away. Indeed, before he could do so, her arms were round him and she was pressing herself against him.

"Are you punishing me for some sin I do not know I have committed?" she asked, her lips raised to his. "I have come to see you, Serle, because I could not bear to be without you any longer. I want you, and I know you want me."

Her arms were round his neck, pulling his head down to hers.

He was not resisting her and was feeling the spell she always exercised over him beginning to work. A second later her lips would have been on his, when the door opened and Freddie came in.

"Hello, Dilys!" he said. "I recognised your carriage outside."

The Marquis disengaged himself from Lady Dilys's clinging arms and she stepped back giving Freddie an undoubtedly baleful glance.

"Did you catch anything?" the Marquis asked.

"Two trout, but they were so small I threw them back," Freddie answered.

He walked to the hearth-rug to look at Dilys with an amused twinkle in his eyes as he said:

"Now why are you here, or need I ask? Were you afraid of Serle getting off the hook?"

"Go away, Freddie, and leave us alone," Lady Dilys said petulantly. "I came to talk to Serle, not to you."

"That of course, I expected, but he is very busy at the moment, and I doubt if he has time for one your special 'talks'."

"He always has time for me," Lady Dilys replied. "Have you not, dearest?"

She put out her hand with its long thin fingers towards the Marquis, but he appeared not to notice.

"I have just been telling Dilys," he said, "that as she cannot stay here tonight, I have suggested that she goes over to the Forsetts."

Lady Dilys laughed, but her eyes were wary.

"I cannot think what you have been doing to Serle," she said to Freddie. "He has gone all respectable, which is something I never expected of him, not if he lived to be a thousand!"

Freddie glanced at the Marquis.

"Serle is right," he said, "although I dare say if you insist on staying we could rustle up a party.

What about asking that pretty girl who has just lost her father?"

If he had intended to annoy Lady Dilys he succeeded.

"What girl?" she asked. "There were no girls at Troon the last time I came here."

"Things change," Freddie answered, "and I am sure if it is a question of emergencies, we could persuade the Dowager to come here for the night. She does not live very far away, and then you and pretty Valeta Lingfield would be properly chaperoned."

Lady Dilys let out a little scream of rage.

"I do not know what you are talking about," she exclaimed, "and who is this Valeta Lingfield anyway?"

"Has Serle not told you that he has acquired a Ward?" Freddie asked. "Sir Charles Lingfield left him his daughter in his Will, and of course, it is a legal obligation he cannot avoid."

Lady Dilys pressed her lips together and looked at the Marquis as if for an explanation, but his eyes were on Freddie's face knowing that his friend was deliberately baiting her and well aware in some subtle way he was getting his own back.

"Freddie is right," the Marquis said decisively. "If you want to stay, Dilys, we must get a party together. I am sure some of my more stodgy neighbours would love to meet you at dinner."

"You are behaving outrageously, as well you

know!" Lady Dilys snapped. "I came here to see you because I could not bear to be without you any longer, and this is the reception I receive!"

"I am sorry," the Marquis replied, "but you should know me well enough by now to be aware that London is one thing and Troon is another."

"I know nothing of the sort!" Lady Dilys replied. "Something has happened to you, something I do not understand. If I go back to London, when will you join me?"

"I am not certain," the Marquis said evasively, "perhaps in a week, it depends when I can complete my arrangements here."

"What arrangements?"

"You would not understand if I told you, but they are, so it happens, important."

"What I suggest," Freddie interposed, "is that you sit down and have some refreshment. I am sure a glass of champagne would be very welcome after your journey. Then when the horses are rested, you can go back to London. You will be there in time for a late dinner."

Dilys looked beseechingly at the Marquis, as if she expected him not to agree to such an outrageous suggestion, but he had his hand on the bell-pull and when a servant appeared at the door, he ordered champagne.

Freddie sat down in a chair next to Dilys and asked conversationally:

"What is the latest gossip from St. James's? If

anything is happening, I am quite certain you know about it."

"Go away, Freddie. Leave us alone," Lady Dilys said. "I want to talk to Serle."

"And I want to talk to you," Freddie said. "In a bachelor establishment such as we have here at the moment, a lovely woman is like a rainbow in the sky!"

He looked round at the Marquis to smile and say:

"That is damned poetical, is it not? Really, I shall have to find myself an 'Incomparable' who will appreciate such a Byronic style."

"You are a bore, Freddie!" Lady Dilys said vehemently. "I have told you to leave me alone with Serle."

"I shall do nothing of the sort!" Freddie replied. "You are only going to try and twist him round into letting you stay here against his better inclinations. Then you will have us at sixes and sevens with each other, which is something I most dislike."

Lady Dilys opened her lips to say something rude, but at that moment a servant entered with the champagne.

They all accepted a glass and as Lady Dilys sipped hers, Freddie said:

"Now tell us if you have done anything outrageous since we last saw you."

Lady Dilys made a little exclamation and said to the Marquis:

"That makes me think of something I came to

tell you and which Freddie put out of my head. I have the most amusing idea for a practical joke."

"If it is like your other ideas in the past," Freddie said before Lady Dilys could go on, "Serle is not to hear it. Has he not told you he has turned over a new leaf and is now taking an interest in his broad acres and his tenants."

"They have managed quite well without him in the past," Lady Dilys retorted.

"That is just where you are wrong," Freddie answered. "They have not. Things have gone sadly awry, and Serle is going to put them to rights, and very efficiently."

"I think the Agent you have found for me will be a great asset," the Marquis said as if he was following his own train of thought. "I was very impressed with his new ideas of harvesting about which he was telling me this morning."

Lady Dilys looked from one man to the other in perplexity.

"Is this true?" she asked after a moment, "are you really becoming interested in farming? You always told me the country bored you except when you were hunting or shooting."

"I think perhaps I missed something in the past," the Marquis replied.

"London is so dull without you, especially now the Regent has gone to Brighton."

"I am surprised you are not there," Freddie remarked.

For a moment Lady Dilys looked embarrassed, then she said quickly:

"I loathe Brighton! The sea winds make my hair so untidy."

Freddie smiled.

He knew now why Lady Dilys was so anxious for the Marquis to return to London.

Most of the *Beau Monde* who surrounded the Prince Regent would be at Brighton, but Lady Dilys had gone too far at the last party at Carlton House when she had offended a number of the Regent's guests and was therefore in his bad books.

While the Regent's private life was outrageous in itself, he always displayed good manners in public and he had grown to dislike practical jokes.

Freddie had not heard the sequel to Lady Dilys's outrageous behaviour which had taken place the night before they had left London for Troon, but now perceptively he was quite certain that she had been told more or less bluntly to stay away from Brighton until she was back in the Regent's favour.

"Personally," he said aloud, "I think that London at this time of year, is hot and boring, and I intend to stay at Troon as long as Serle will have me."

"That is what I would like too," Lady Dilys said, "and I can hardly believe it possible that he should refuse to have me when I have driven all this way just to see him."

She bent forward in her chair, her face raised towards the Marquis who was standing with his back to the fireplace, a glass of champagne in his hand.

"Let me stay with you, Serle," she said pleadingly. "We will have such fun, and you know that I love you!"

It would have been difficult for any man to resist the appeal in her voice and the beauty of her face, and it seemed as if for a moment, both the Marquis and Freddie were hypnotised into stillness. Then the Marquis replied:

"If you insist on staying, Dilys, I will send a groom to my mother to ask her to join us, or if she cannot do so, I am sure she could spare her companion, a most respectable elderly widow."

Lady Dilys put her empty glass down with a slight slap on the table.

"I have no intention of staying where I am not wanted! Ponsonby is in London, so is Sinclair, and George Weston. They will look after me, and I am sure we shall find some amusement which do not smell of pigs or freshly manured ground!"

Her voice had a bitter fury which was unmistakable.

She rose to her feet with a rustle of silk and sweeping past the Marquis and Freddie walked down the room.

It was a dramatic exit, but both men were well aware knowing Lady Dilys as they did, that she expected them to stop her long before she reached the door.

The Marquis's eyes met those of his friend and

Freddie knew without a word being spoken that he was being told to let her go.

They caught up with her only when Lady Dilys had reached the Hall and still without speaking a word she descended the steps to where her carriage was waiting.

A servant opened the door and handed her in and the Marquis and Freddie stood side by side on the top of the steps.

As the coachman drove the horses away they had a last glimpse of Lady Dilys's profile silhouetted in all its beauty against the dark background of the carriage. Then she was moving away from them down the drive.

Freddie put up his hand to his forehead as if he expected it to be wet with sweat and as they walked silently across the Hall and into the Library he said:

"God knows, Serle, I never thought you had it in you to turn down Dilys in such a manner. What happened before I came into the room?"

"She asked me to marry her."

"And you refused?"

"Of course. I do not intend ever to marry."

"That is nonsense, but at least it is not Dilys."

"No, and it was you who persuaded me it would not be practical."

"It would not be a great many other things," Freddie muttered. "I feel that I have pulled you back from a bottomless abyss."

"I suppose that is true," the Marquis said reflectively. "Do you know, Freddie, it is a

damned queer thing, but I suddenly realised —
and I cannot explain it even to myself — she no
longer attracts me."

"I felt like that a long time ago," Freddie replied, "and I can only thank God, and I mean
that in all sincerity, that you found out in time."

"Yes, I found out in time," the Marquis said.
"What puzzles me is why it should have happened so suddenly in the way it has?"

"Perhaps you will never know the answer,"
Freddie said cheerfully, "but whatever it is, let
us drink to our freedom! By God, I need a drink
at this moment!"

CHAPTER FIVE

By the time her carriage had reached the end of the drive Lady Dilys was shaking with anger.

She could not believe it possible that the Marquis had not prevented her from leaving.

On other occasions she had threatened a dramatic exit to gain her own way and had always been prevented from leaving at the last moment.

Once, she remembered, the gentleman in question had run after her coach and sprang into it when it was actually moving quite quickly to seat himself beside the fair charmer who had captured his heart.

On that occasion she had allowed the carriage to travel for nearly a mile before she had with a well-simulated reluctance given orders for her horses to be turned round.

Incredibly the Marquis had not followed her and she had the uncomfortable feeling that she might never see him again.

She had, in fact, been slightly perturbed, but not overwhelmingly so, when the Marquis had not returned to London and to her side as quickly as she had expected.

When he had left London she was quite certain it would be a question of his being away only a day or two, then irresistibly she would have drawn him back by the strong, fiery passion that linked them to each other.

That the Marquis could suddenly become immune to her blandishments, that he could assume an indifference to her pleading that she might stay with him, seemed so unlikely that Lady Dilys could not credit it had really occurred.

But as her horses plodded on, passing through the dusty lanes to reach the Highway, she told herself almost despairingly that she had lost the one man who mattered at this moment more in her life than any others.

She had made up her mind to marry the Marquis, not only because he was the richest and most important of any of her lovers, but also because he genuinely attracted her.

She liked his recklessness which echoed her own, his daring and his spirit of fun, which made him so different in temperament from her other suitors.

She had decided some time ago, that she would marry him. There had however seemed no need for haste until after the scene at Carlton House, where she had learnt with some dismay that if she went to Brighton, the Regent would not acknowledge her presence there.

Lady Dilys admitted to herself frankly that she had gone too far and had not only antagonised the Regent himself, but far more dangerous, aroused the animosity of Lady Conyngham.

While Lady Dilys believed she could do anything with any man who was not blind, she knew that where women were concerned it was a very different story.

Women mistrusted and disapproved of her and, as Lady Conyngham had supplanted Lady Hertford in the Regent's affections and he was becoming more and more infatuated with her, there was no doubt that her approval was very important to those who wished to be invited either to Carlton House or to the Royal Pavilion at Brighton.

To be in Brighton and not take part in the huge dinner parties and musical soirees that took place almost nightly in the Royal Pavilion, was to be little better than a pariah.

However daring Lady Dilys might be, at the moment she had not the courage to brave Social ostracism in Brighton.

She therefore told herself that the obvious course was to marry the Marquis immediately.

"She had known perceptively, because she was well experienced where men were concerned, that he was thinking of asking her to be his wife.

The words had, she was sure, trembled on his lips on one or two occasions without his actually uttering them, but Lady Dilys had thought triumphantly that it was only a question of time.

But now time was something she could not afford and she therefore decided that as the Marquis had not returned to London she would go to Troon.

She was quite sure that before she left Troon they would be betrothed and after that no-one in the length and breath of the land would bar their doors to her.

What was more, because the Regent was genuinely fond of the Marquis his wife would be forgiven any misdeeds she might have committed in the past, and as the Marchioness of Troon she would be able to rule the *Beau Monde* from an unassailable social position with unlimited wealth to support it.

The more she thought about it the more attractive the idea seemed and the more she was determined the nuptial day should be fixed.

There were quite a number of protests from her adoring swains before she left London.

Despite the fact that they all knew she was the Marquis's acknowledged mistress, they had either enjoyed Lady Dilys's favours in the past or hoped to do so in the future.

She had quite a gratifying send off when she left the house in Curzon Street to drive to Troon.

Now she had the suspicion that they would speculate privately amongst themselves, if they dared not speak about it openly, as to why she had returned without the Marquis and with no promise, unless she invented one, of when he would be back in London.

"How could I have lost him?" Lady Dilys asked.

How could it have happened? How could any man, who had been as infatuated with her as the Marquis had been, suddenly become cold and aloof and indifferent when she had pressed her body against his and put her arms round his neck.

Something had changed him, she thought — but what? — Or who?

Carefully Lady Dilys went over every word that had been spoken since she had arrived at Troon.

She had known that Freddie was baiting her and she had been aware for some time, that he disliked her association with the Marquis.

Not because he was jealous — that she could have understood — but because his affection for his friend made him consider her a bad influence.

She had suspected in the past, she thought, that Freddie was really an enemy, but now he had shown her his true colours and she thought that if only she was a man, it would give her real pleasure to shoot him down and see him dying at her feet.

"I will get even with him one day," she promised herself, but knew her problem at the moment was not Freddie, but the Marquis.

If he would not marry her — and she had the uncomfortable feeling that was now very likely — to whom could she turn?

Lord Ponsonby, who had pursued her for years, whilst being an attractive man, had no money.

In fact, the only wealthy member of her circle at the moment was Sir George Weston, who might be extremely rich but was an unmitigated bore, both in bed and out.

Lady Dilys clenched her fingers until the knuckles showed white.

"How can I have lost Serle?" she muttered to herself. "He loves me, I know he loves me!"

But she could see again the expression in his eyes when she had pleaded with him and knew that in some extraordinary manner, he had withdrawn from her into a distant land where she could not reach him.

Then suddenly like a flash of lightning she remembered Freddie's talk of the pretty girl who had become the Marquis's Ward.

Vaguely she remembered that on previous visits to Troon she had met a good-looking, older man called Sir Charles Lingfield, who she had learned was a near neighbour.

She had not wasted any time with him, but the men she met were always stored in Lady Dilys's mind, just in case in the future they ever came in useful.

She thought over what she had heard; Sir Charles Lingfield had for some reason that was not explained, made his daughter the Marquis's Ward.

Could she be the reason for the change in the man that Lady Dilys had felt she knew so intimately, but who had in a few days, become almost a stranger?

Still it did not seem possible because the Marquis had always disliked girls and found them gauche and uninteresting, although actually despite the manoeuvring of ambitious mothers he had met very few of them.

"Valeta Lingfield!" Lady Dilys repeated almost under her breath.

There was a venomous expression in her eyes which would certainly have alarmed Valeta had she seen it.

The carriage proceeded at a good pace towards London until they began to encounter increased traffic on the outskirts.

As the Marquis had chosen and paid for the horses that filled Lady Dilys's stable, the journey was not as arduous as it would have been with inferior animals.

In fact, deep in her thoughts Lady Dilys was surprised when she realised they were not only inside the Metropolis but proceeding down Park Lane.

It was then she bent forward almost automatically to look at Stevington House.

She had been so sure when she passed it this morning on her way to Troon, that she would soon be its mistress and give parties as the Marquis's mother had done, in the great Ballroom, but for what Lady Dilys called 'much more amusing people'.

Now she told herself with a renewal of her anger that the picture of herself standing at the top of the stairs with the Marquis beside her was likely to exist only in her imagination and never become a reality.

Stevington House silhouetted against the last glow of the setting sun looked magnificent and had a grandeur that made it seem to eclipse all the other grand houses in the aristocratic road which overlooked Hyde Park.

It was then that Lady Dilys saw a familiar figure standing outside the house.

It was not hard to recognise Lionel Stevington, for he had an undeniable resemblance to his brother even though the expression on his face, bitter and cynical made him unattractive and caused a number of his acquaintances to pretend not to have seen him or pass him with an indifferent nod.

He was standing now talking to a large, rough-looking man and Lady Dilys thought with a curl of her lip that he was doubtless abusing his brother while in reality he would give anything in the world to be the owner of Stevington House and Troon.

Lady Dilys was too experienced with men not to realise that Lionel's pretence of 'helping the under-dog' sprang merely from envy, hatred and malice.

She had often warned the Marquis laughingly that one night Lionel would stab him in the back in some dark alley, and the following morning step into his shoes with alacrity.

The carriage had almost passed Stevington House when Lady Dilys peremptorily ordered it to stop.

The coachman drew the horses to a standstill

127

and when the footman jumped down from the box to enquire her wishes she said:

"Ask the gentleman who is standing over there, to come and speak to me."

The footman hurried to obey her and she sat back in the carriage waiting, her eyes narrowing a little, her full lips set in a hard line.

"And what can Your Ladyship want of a poor unimportant fellow like myself?" a mocking voice asked at the window.

"Get in!" Lady Dilys said curtly.

Lionel Stevington raised his eye-brows, but the footman opened the door and he obeyed her, seating himself beside her on the back seat and throwing his high hat on the one opposite him.

It was typical that despite his alleged *penchant* for the working classes, he continued to dress as a gentleman of fashion, knowing that it made his revolutionary and radical prejudices sound more forceful when he did not look the part.

He leaned back very much at his ease and contemplated Lady Dilys in a manner which she knew was deliberately insulting, but which for the moment she was not prepared to challenge.

"Were you calling at Stevington House to see your brother?" she enquired.

"Of course."

"May I ask why?"

"It is no secret," he replied. "I am merely asking for some of the crumbs that fall from the table, or should I say the bed, of lovely creatures like yourself."

Lady Dilys ignored the rudeness.

"You are misinformed," she said. "Your brother is not spending his money on me at the moment, but on someone else!"

She saw that Lionel Stevington was surprised, but also interested.

"I thought you had His Lordship thoroughly tied up."

"So did I," Lady Dilys replied, "but I was mistaken."

"You amaze me," Lionel remarked.

"It has amazed me too," Lady Dilys agreed. "But I thought you should be the first to know, since it concerns you so closely, that your brother is in danger of being lured into matrimony with a young girl."

"Matrimony?"

Lionel Stevington stiffened.

Lady Dilys knew that he had never imagined there was any likelihood of such a union between herself and the Marquis.

"Yes, matrimony," she said, "for it is unlikely that he could offer any other position to Sir Charles Lingfield's daughter."

There was a frown between Lionel Stevington's eyes as he said:

"I remember Lingfield, but I had no idea he had a daughter."

"She is now your brother's Ward, and I am told, very pretty."

Lady Dilys thought to herself that her voice seemed to hiss the words as she spoke them, but she had the feeling that in some way, she was not quite certain how, she was striking back at the Marquis.

"Tell me about this girl," Lionel Stevington said after a moment.

Lady Dilys shrugged her shoulders.

"I was naturally not allowed to see her," she said. "I was only told of her existence and how preoccupied your brother is with her. In fact, in consequence, I was sent away from Troon, as if I was a servant no longer required, something I have not experienced until now."

He heard the chagrin in her voice and laughed.

"So Serle has turned you off, has he?" he asked. "Well, I expect you have had some good pickings off him, and I dare say there will be plenty of other fellows to take his place."

He leant forward to retrieve his hat from the seat opposite him as he added:

"I am obliged to you for the information."

"I thought it would please you to know that you could quite soon become an uncle," Lady Dilys said, "and after all, you have never had any real chance of inheriting the title. Your brother is young and very attractive."

Lionel Stevington knew that she was being spiteful because for a moment, he had got under her skin.

Again he laughed, and opening the carriage door, stepped out.

"I wish Your Ladyship good-day and good hunting!"

The innuendo in his words made Lady Dilys want to spit at him. Instead she watched him walk jauntily away back to where the large rough-looking man was still waiting.

As she drove on towards her own house, she wondered if she had gained anything by her conversation with Lionel Stevington.

She had the infuriating feeling that he in fact, had been more insolent to her than she had to him, and yet she might have struck a blow at the Marquis — she was not sure.

If Serle was unpredictable, so was his brother, and at the moment she loathed them both.

The Marquis received a note early the following morning from his mother to say how she longed to see him and would be delighted to meet Valeta Lingfield again, whom she had known as a small child.

But she unfortunately could not invite them to luncheon until the following day.

"I have promised for a long time," she wrote in her beautiful upright hand-writing, *"to take luncheon with your Aunt Dorothea. As She is over eighty, I would not like to inconvenience Her by changing My plans at the last moment. I know, dearest Boy, that you will understand and I look forward to seeing You on Thursday with little Valeta, and will expect You both here at a half after twelve o'clock."*

131

The Marquis gave the information contained in his mother's note to Freddie as they breakfasted together.

"I will have to drive over and tell Valeta that I will take her tomorrow instead of today," he said. "It will not take me long. Are you coming with me?"

"No, I want to read the newspapers," Freddie answered. "When you come back I want you to come and look at that horse of mine. Archer says he is definitely off-colour but can find no reason for it."

"If Archer does not know what is wrong," the Marquis replied, "the trouble either exists in your imagination, or it is really serious."

"I hope it is not that," Freddie said. "I paid a large sum for my team and I certainly cannot afford to lose any of them."

"I should not worry too much," the Marquis said, "I expect it is only a temporary indisposition. Some horses hate the heat."

"That may be the explanation," his friend said, "but I would still like you to look at him."

"Of course I will do that," the Marquis answered. "I must just tell Valeta not to put on her best bib and tucker until tomorrow."

He finished his breakfast and set off immediately driving a light Phaeton with a pair of perfectly matched horses that moved together in a manner which always gave the Marquis pleasure every time he handled them.

It took him only about ten minutes to reach

the Manor House and he thought as he drove down the overgrown drive that Valeta would very likely be delighted that she did not have to endure his company on the long drive to his mother's, but could postpone the irksome experience until the following day.

The Marquis knew without conceit that most women would give almost anything for the pleasure and excitement of driving alone with him anywhere he wished to go.

He wondered what his mother would make of Valeta, seeing that she was in every way different from anyone he had taken to meet her on previous occasions.

But those he had taken to luncheon or tea with the Dowager Marchioness had not included Lady Dilys.

He knew that to his mother she would not have been a welcome guest, and one reason why he had not proposed marriage to Dilys was the knowledge that his mother would disapprove of her as his wife and would have been much upset by the thought of Dilys taking what had been her place at Troon.

"Mama will be glad that I am going to see her for a very different reason," the Marquis thought.

A turn in the drive revealed the Manor House ahead.

As the Marquis drew his horses up at the front door Valeta's old Nurse came running out through the doorway in a manner that told him before she spoke that she was upset.

"Oh, M'Lord, M'Lord!" she cried. "Thank God you are here! I was just about to send for Your Lordship — and now you've come!"

Her voice sounded so strange and her words were so incoherent that the Marquis quickly threw down the reins and as his groom went to the heads of his horses, stepped out of the Phaeton.

"What is the matter?" he enquired. "What has Nicholas been doing?"

"It's not Nicholas, M'Lord," Nannie gasped. "It's Miss Valeta! Oh, M'Lord, they've taken her away!"

"Taken her away?" the Marquis asked.

He had moved automatically through the front door into the small hall, and now he looked at the old Nurse in perplexity as the words came tumbling from her.

"Two men, M'Lord. They snatched her up and little Harry as she was a-talking to, covered them with cloths, threw them into a carriage and drove off."

Nanny was gasping for breath before she finished speaking and her hands were shaking in a manner which made the Marquis feel she might collapse.

Firmly he took her by the arm and sat her down on the seat at the bottom of the stairs.

"Now start from the beginning," he said quietly, "and tell me exactly what happened."

"Oh, M'Lord, 'twas terrible!" Nanny murmured.

"From the beginning!" the Marquis said firmly. "Where were you when this happened?"

"I was in the Drawing-Room, M'Lord," Nanny began, and the Marquis realised it was a great effort for her to speak more slowly.

"What were you doing?" he asked.

"I was brushing the carpet, M'Lord, and Miss Valeta was arranging the flowers."

She gave a gasp of breath before she continued:

"There was a knock on the door and Miss Valeta says to me: 'I will go, Nanny,' and she walks across the hall. I hears her speak to Nicholas as she passed him."

"He was in the hall?" the Marquis questioned.

"Yes, M'Lord, playing with some old toys Miss Valeta had found for him in the attic."

"Then what happened?"

"I heard Miss Valeta say: 'Good-morning, Harry! I see you have brought us some butter.' "

"Who is Harry?"

"He's the little boy from the Home Farm, M'Lord. We always buys the butter from Mr. Hopson and he sends it to us fresh from the churn twice a week."

"What happened then?" the Marquis asked.

"Miss Valeta calls to me, M'Lord: 'Harry is here, Nanny. Is there anything we want? Have we enough eggs?' and I says:

" 'We'd better have a dozen tomorrow.' You see, M'Lord, since we've had Nicholas with us, we've been trying to make him eat . . ."

"Never mind about that now," the Marquis said. "Go on with what occurred."

"I was continuing with my brushing, M'Lord, when I hears Nicholas give a sudden shriek.

" 'They've come for me!' he cried. 'They've come! Save me! Save me!'

"I hears him running upstairs as quick as his legs could carry him."

"What did you do?" the Marquis asked.

"Thinking it was strange I put down my pan and brush and went into the hall to see what had upset him, and as I did so I heard Miss Valeta give a cry. It were a cry of fear, M'Lord."

"What was happening? Could you see?"

"Yes, M'Lord. There was a cloth over her head and a man were carrying her in his arms into a carriage that was standing outside the door."

"What sort of carriage?"

"I couldn't rightly say, M'Lord. 'Twas closed and was a bit old and dark, somehow."

"And they put Miss Valeta into it?" the Marquis asked.

"I sees the man push her into it, M'Lord, and another man was carrying young Harry, also with a cloth or sack over his head. He just throws him in and as I runs forward, having been so astonished I was unable to move, so to speak, they drives off!"

"There was another man on the box?"

"Yes, M'Lord. A coachman, but not in livery, or anything like that. Leastways, I don't think so."

"How many horses?" the Marquis asked.

Nanny thought for a moment.

"Two I think, but I'm not certain. I was looking at the carriage door thinking I might see Miss Valeta, but it was dark, and I couldn't see her, and I couldn't believe it had all happened."

"No, of course not," the Marquis agreed.

Tears were running down the old Nurse's face and now she put her hands to her eyes as if she was completely overwhelmed.

"Where is Nicholas?" the Marquis asked after a moment.

Nanny's voice was only a croak broken with tears as she answered:

"I expects he's under Miss Valeta's bed, M'Lord. It's where he always hides when he's frightened."

The Marquis went up the stairs two at a time.

He had to guess which of three doors opened off the landing into Valeta's bedroom, and opening the first door found he had made a mistake for the blinds were drawn and the bed was covered in dust-sheets.

He went to the next room and found the sun pouring in through the window.

There was a bed with a white muslin flounce matching the muslin skirt which enveloped the dressing-table.

It was, he thought, very much a young girl's room and smelt of lavender and roses, and was very different in every way from the bedrooms in which the Marquis had sported himself with women like Lady Dilys.

There was no sound except the song of the birds outside and the buzzing of a bee which had settled on some roses which stood in a vase on the dressing-table.

Then he heard a little whimper which he had heard before and knew who had made it.

"It is all right, Nicholas," he said quietly, "there is nothing to frighten you. I want you to come out and talk to me."

There was no response and the Marquis bent down and lifting the flounce looked under the bed.

There was a faint scream of terror and he saw Nicholas curled up like a small ball pressed against the wall.

"Listen, Nicholas," the Marquis said, "I need your help, and I need it very quickly."

"They will . . . take me . . . away!" Nicholas cried, and the Marquis could hear the terror in his voice. "They will take me . . . away and . . . burn my feet!"

"Who will take you away?" the Marquis asked.

There was no answer and he knew the child was terrified almost beyond words.

The Marquis knelt down on one knee as he had done before.

"Please help me, Nicholas," he said. "Those wicked people have taken Miss Lingfield away and unless you want them to harm her I have to find her very quickly. So you must please help me."

The small boy had hidden his head in his

arms. Now the Marquis saw his eyes peeping at him and he went on:

"You do not want them to hurt Miss Lingfield, and I must know where they have gone. Come and tell me what you saw. Please, Nicholas."

For a moment the Marquis thought he had failed. Then Nicholas began to crawl towards him.

He came out from the flounce under the bed and then swiftly like a small animal that seeks sanctuary, he threw himself against the Marquis, putting his arms round his neck and holding onto him so tightly that the Marquis found it hard to breathe.

Slowly, so that the child did not become more frightened than he was already, he got to his feet, lifting him in his arms.

"No-one is going to hurt you," he said soothingly. "Look out of the window and you will see that the men have gone away. There is no-one there."

He carried the child to the window so that he could look down on the empty drive beneath them.

"You see — they have gone!" the Marquis said. "But they have taken Miss Lingfield with them and I have to catch up with them. So tell me, Nicholas, who they were."

Against his ear so softly that the Marquis could hardly hear, Nicholas whispered:

"I saw — Bill!"

"Who is Bill?"

"He — beat me and he — stuck pins into my — feet!"

The arms round the Marquis's neck clutched convulsively, but he managed to say:

"That is something he shall never do again, I promise you that."

He knew now what he had already guessed, that the men who had carried Valeta off had something to do with Cibber, but it seemed peculiar that they should have taken a strange boy with them, unless . . .

The Marquis carried Nicholas downstairs to find Nanny still sitting on the chair in the hall.

"What does the boy Harry look like, Nanny?" he asked as she rose a little uncertainly to her feet.

"He's got fair hair, M'Lord, and is nicely spoken."

"How old is he?"

"I don't rightly know, M'Lord, perhaps seven or eight years of age."

"And he looks something like Nicholas?"

"I wouldn't say that, M'Lord, except that they're both fair."

The Marquis was certain in his mind that Harry had been taken by mistake for Nicholas.

Aloud he said:

"I want you and Nicholas to come with me to Troon while I go and find Miss Lingfield."

"Oh, M'Lord, that's what I hoped you'd say. You'll bring her back, won't you? It's a-feared I am for her in the hands of those men."

"I will bring her back, Nanny," the Marquis said quietly. "You may be sure of that. But there is no time to be lost."

He saw Nanny look round as if she intended to fetch things and he said firmly:

"Come just as you are. We can send for anything you need later. I think Nicholas should feel he is safe, which he will not do while he is here."

Without waiting for Nanny to acquiesce the Marquis walked out of the front door with Nicholas in his arms and set him down in the Phaeton.

The child seemed for a moment reluctant to take his arms from around his neck, then the excitement at being high off the ground and driving behind two horses took his attention for the moment from his own personal fear.

Nanny climbed up beside him and they drove off with Nicholas sandwiched in between her and the Marquis.

The Marquis proceeded at a much quicker rate than he had on his journey from Troon.

He was trying to calculate what had happened and for what reason Valeta had been spirited away, presumably by Cibber. He had thought the man was quite satisfied with the money he had handed over in exchange for Nicholas.

It had, in fact, been far in excess of what an ordinary apprentice might pay to be released from his bond, but the Marquis was aware that Cibber had resented being beaten by a woman and he supposed this was in some extraordinary way his revenge.

They reached the main drive. Troon lay ahead of them magnificent with its windows glistening and the lake golden with sunshine at its feet.

The Marquis felt a sudden tremor pass through Nicholas and felt the small boy draw even closer to him than he was already.

"It is all right," he said looking down at him with a smile. "You will be quite safe here."

"Chimneys," Nicholas murmured, "lots and lots of — chimneys."

"Do not worry about them," the Marquis said, "and there will never be another climbing boy in them again."

The way he spoke surprised even himself, and he thought with a twist of his lips that Valeta had won a victory and would be delighted that he had capitulated to her demands.

Then he told himself that before she could learn of his decision he would have to find her, and it now struck him more forcibly that it might prove extremely difficult to do so.

He drew the horses up outside the front door and said to the groom:

"Go to the stables and tell them I require immediately my racing Phaeton and the new chestnut team to draw it."

"Very good, M'Lord."

The Marquis lifted Nicholas down to the ground and walking up the steps said to Andrews:

142

"Fetch Mr. Chamberlain and Mrs. Fielding. Where is Captain Weyborne?"

"In the Library, M'Lord."

"Tell all three I want them."

Footmen went hurrying in every direction and the Marquis stood waiting in the centre of the Hall, still holding Nicholas by the hand.

Mr. Chamberlain appeared from below the stairs as Mrs. Fielding appeared at the top of them and there was a surprised expression on both their faces as they hurried towards the Marquis.

"Nurse and the small boy are to stay here, and the latter is to be assured that he is in no danger and no-one will hurt him."

"Hurt him?" Mr. Chamberlain questioned.

"Miss Lingfield has been abducted, and a boy from the Home Farm who was talking to her and whom I am convinced they mistook for Nicholas, has been taken with her."

While Mr. Chamberlain's mouth opened in astonishment Freddie had come into the Hall and unnoticed by the Marquis had reached his side.

"What are you saying, Serle?" he enquired. "Valeta has been abducted. It cannot be possible!"

"It is very possible," the Marquis answered, "and Nicholas recognised one of the men who took her away as a man called Bill, who is in Cibber's employment."

"The Sweep?"

"Exactly!"

The Marquis turned again to Mr. Chamberlain.

"You have Cibber's address?"

"Yes, of course, My Lord. He sweeps the chimneys at Stevington House. That is why he came to Troon."

"From London?" the Marquis asked in surprise.

"No local Sweep could take on anything so large as this house," Mr. Chamberlain explained, "and as the chimneys had to be swept, I arranged for Cibber to come here."

"I see . . ." the Marquis said. "I never thought he might be a London man."

As he spoke he realised that this made it all the more urgent for him to find Valeta quickly.

"Give me Cibber's address," he said sharply, "and Freddie, we will take a couple of pistols with us."

"I cannot imagine what is going on," Freddie replied.

"This is no time for words," the Marquis said firmly. Then to the Housekeeper he said: "Take Nurse upstairs. See that she and the little boy are comfortable. You can send someone later in the day to collect their things from the Manor House."

"They are to stay here, M'Lord?"

"Until I return," the Marquis replied.

"And you'll bring Miss Valeta with you?" Nanny asked in a voice that broke. "Pray God, M'Lord, you'll be able to do that."

"I feel sure I will be able to," the Marquis replied firmly, "Look after Nicholas. He has been very frightened."

Nanny put out her hand to Nicholas but the small boy suddenly flung his arms round the Marquis's leg.

"I want to come with you," he said. "I'll be safe with you."

"You will be safe here until I come back," the Marquis answered, "and I think if you are very good, Mr. Chamberlain might be able to find a pony for you to ride."

"Like Rufus?"

"You must tell me if he is like Rufus," the Marquis answered.

He did not realise that hearing the gentle and understanding manner in which he was speaking to Nicholas, both his Comptroller and his friend were looking at him in astonishment.

The small boy loosened his grip of the Marquis's leg.

"You will be back very soon, won't you?" he asked wistfully.

"Just as soon as I can find Miss Lingfield for you."

"I'll be praying, M'Lord, I'll be praying every moment you are gone," Nanny cried. "Oh, how can this have happened? My poor baby! My poor baby!"

The Marquis glanced at the Housekeeper who put her arms round Nanny and began to draw her up the stairs.

Mr. Chamberlain took Nicholas by the hand.

"Suppose we go and look for that pony now," he said, and saw an expression of delight replace the one of fear in the small boy's eyes.

The Marquis turned to Freddie.

"You are ready?" he asked.

"These are the pistols you require," the Butler said stepping forward, "and here is that man Cibber's address. He left a card in the Pantry, M'Lord, when he was here last."

"It is the last thing he will ever leave in this house," the Marquis said grimly.

He took the card from the Butler.

It was a trade card such as many tradesmen had printed, to present to their patrons even though the 'Sweeps and their like could not read.

The Marquis read:

"CIBBER
Chimney Sweeper & Nightman
9 Duck Lane
St. Giles
Begs leave most respectfully to inform his Friends and the Public in general, that he continues to sweep Chimnies of all Descriptions, cleans Smoke Jacks, Smokey Coppers, and extinguishes Chimnies when on Fire, with the greatest Care and Safety.

———

SMOKEY CHIMNIES CURED
Drains and Sesspools cleaned on the Shortest Notice.
CHIMNIES SWEPT BY THE YEAR."

Andrews now held out to Freddie the duelling

146

pistols in their polished box.

Freddie put one in his own pocket and handed the other to the Marquis who was still looking at the card he held in his hand.

"St. Giles'!" he murmured, and he was thinking as he spoke that he could not imagine a more terrible place for Valeta to be taken.

Anyone who lived in London was aware of the horrors that took place in the district of St. Giles' where there were a number of "Flash Houses," that even the Police avoided and would not enter unless in a band.

The Marquis had heard that over four hundred delinquents slept in one of the houses where the inmates were trained in crime from their very earliest teens.

The boys gradually becoming expert went out thieving, pilfering, picking pockets, injuring and even murdering those who resisted them, while the girls, who might be only twelve or thirteen years old, became prostitutes.

The Marquis had, in fact, read a report by one of the Select Committees of what happened in the "Flash Houses" and he could only hope this was not one that had come to Valeta's notice.

He knew that the horror and traffic of the "Flash Houses" would appal any woman who was gently bred.

He thrust the card into his pocket, took the second duelling-pistol, and walked towards the door.

As he did so the Phaeton he had ordered,

drawn by a superb team of chestnuts which he had bought only a few months before at Tattersall's, came hurrying round from the stables.

The horses were fresh and it was difficult for the grooms to hold them while the Marquis climbed into the high driving-seat and Freddie joined him.

They moved off, driving from the very outset with a speed that made Freddie aware of the Marquis's sense of urgency to save Valeta from what they were both aware might well be a fate very much worse than death!

CHAPTER SIX

Valeta was at first, so helpless with the cloth over her head and shaken by the roughness with which she had been flung down onto the seat of the carriage, that it was difficult to breathe, let alone think.

Then as she heard and felt the wheels turning beneath her and heard Harry begin to cry from fright, she put up her hands to pull the cloth from her head.

"Leave it be!" a rough voice said, "or Oi'll toi yer up!"

She realised then there was a man sitting opposite her on the seat of the carriage with his back to the horses, and for a moment the harshness of his voice and the threat he had uttered made her speechless.

She tried to recall what had happened.

She had been talking to Harry when she had heard the sound of an approaching vehicle and seen two horses come round the curve of the drive.

She had thought it must be the Marquis and she felt, as always when he approached, a sudden constriction within her which she could not prevent.

Then as she looked at the horses she realised they were certainly not the type of animal the Marquis would drive and she wondered which

149

tradesman they belonged to and why he should be calling on them when, as far as she knew, Nanny had ordered nothing.

Then the carriage which the horses were drawing came into view and she saw the driver of it was a rough-looking man with a cap pulled low over his forehead and a red handkerchief tied round his neck.

She watched the vehicle approach with curiosity and was just about to tell Harry that she wanted nothing more and he could go home when the carriage was brought to a standstill, the door of it opened and out jumped two men.

They rushed up to her, and before she could realise what was happening she was in darkness with a cloth over her head and was being carried forcibly in strong arms to be flung violently onto the seat of the carriage.

A second or so later she heard Harry cry as he was thrown down beside her.

Valeta struggling to think clearly tried to imagine what had happened and for what reason she was being carried off in such a manner.

She knew by now the carriage must have reached the end of the drive and had turned onto the road that led through the village.

She wondered if she screamed loudly enough or perhaps managed to reach the window whether any of the villagers would come to her assistance.

Then she had the uncomfortable feeling that long before she could attract attention the man who had spoken so roughly and was sitting opposite her, would force her into silence.

She did not like to think of the methods he might use to obtain it.

So she merely sat back in the seat knowing the carriage was a poor one, badly upholstered, and the wheels turning beneath her jolted and bumped in a manner which told her that any springing was non-existent.

"What will happen to me?" she asked herself and was afraid of the answer.

They must have driven for a mile and Valeta was now aware that they were out of the village and not far from the Highway. In a quiet and what she hoped was a conciliatory tone she said:

"Would it be possible for me to remove this cloth from my face as it is making me so hot and it is hard to breathe."

There was silence for a moment, then the man said grudgingly:

"Oi s'pose it'll be orl right, but if yer shouts or tries to attrac' attention Oi'll clobber yer!"

That, Valeta thought, was what she had expected him to do and she raised the cloth tentatively just to be certain he would not change his mind, then pulled it from her head.

Sitting opposite her was an exceedingly unpleasant-looking character.

He was a young man, she thought, of about twenty years or more. His features were coarse, his skin was pockmarked and he was extremely dirty.

He wore a cloth cap pulled low on his forehead

and there was a torn handkerchief round his neck.

He was looking at her in a speculative manner which made her feel afraid, and she instinctively put her hands to her hair to tidy it, then looked down at Harry.

He was crying beneath the piece of sacking that covered him and which Valeta saw was ingrained with soot.

"May I take this off the boy?" she asked.

"Oi s'pose so," the man said grudgingly.

She pulled away the dirty sacking and threw it down on the floor. Then as Harry's frightened, tear-stained face looked up at her she heard the man opposite ejaculate:

" 'E ain't Nichilas!"

"No, of course not," Valeta said. "This is Harry, a local farmer's son, and I promise you there will be a great hue and cry when his father realises he is missing!"

"Oi wants to go back to me Pa!" Harry cried, his sobs breaking out afresh.

"Do not cry," Valeta said. "There has been a mistake and you should not be here at all."

She looked down at the soot-covered canvas on the floor, then at the man who was staring at Harry as if he could not believe his eyes, and said accusingly:

"It was Nicholas you were trying to kidnap, was it not?"

" 'E be like Nichilas," the man answered, as if excusing himself.

"Then as you have made a mistake," Valeta said. "I suggest you stop the carriage and put us down on the roadway. We will find our own way home."

" 'E be like Nichilas," the man said again.

"But he is not Nicholas," Valeta said firmly as if speaking to a child. "Therefore you have made a mistake in bringing him here. If in fact, you intended to kidnap Nicholas, it was exceedingly dishonest, considering His Lordship bought his apprenticeship."

It was obvious to Valeta that Cibber the Sweep had regretted his bargain and had not only accepted the money which the Marquis had paid him for Nicholas, but was now trying to steal the child back.

Although she knew Harry was frightened and she was sorry for the little boy, she could not help feeling an irrepressible gladness that it was not in fact Nicholas who was being subjected to a further ordeal at the hands of the man who had already treated him so badly.

It was only last night that she had said to Nanny after putting Nicholas to bed:

"Another child might have gone mad, being treated in such an inhuman manner."

"It's something that'll never happen again," Nanny answered, "and time will heal the agony of it in his mind."

"I hope so," Valeta said.

Twice the night before she had got up to go to Nicholas when he had cried out in his sleep.

Although Nanny wanted to have him with her, Valeta felt that he was her own special charge, and she therefore put him into the small dressing-room which led off the bedroom in which she slept.

By leaving the communicating door open she could actually see him lying in bed, and when she heard him turning and tossing and murmuring in his sleep, she had held him close in her arms and soothed him until he was no longer frightened.

To think of these monsters trying to take the child back again seemed a wickedness beyond anything she could imagine.

But with an effort she forced a smile to her lips as she said to the man opposite:

"Now you see it has all been a great mistake, so will you attract the attention of your friends, and tell them there has been a mix-up?"

As she spoke she was calculating in her mind that the moment she got back she must send for the Marquis and they must take Nicholas away to safety.

If Cibber wanted him so much he might try to kidnap him again, and she could not help feeling that the only place where Nicholas would be safe would be at Troon.

She thought the man opposite was going to respond to her plea, when he said with a grin that somehow was exceedingly unpleasant:

"Us might 'ave made a mistike about 'im, but not about ye!"

154

"Me?" Valeta questioned. "But why should you wish to kidnap me?"

"That's tellin'!"

Valeta looked at him wide-eyed.

"Is it possible that somebody has sent you not only to take Nicholas back to his cruel master, but also to abduct me? It cannot be true!"

"It be rite 'nough Ye're wanted — that's wot yer are!"

Valeta remembered how she had defied the Sweep and the angry glance he had given her before the Marquis sent him from the room.

So this was his revenge!

Yet it did not seem possible somehow that any man engaged in a trade, however lowly, would dare to risk transportation, which was the punishment for abduction.

Then it struck her that perhaps he intended to use her to extort money from the Marquis as a ransom and she felt how uncomfortable such a situation would be, and how humiliating.

"I may be very stupid," she said aloud, "but I cannot understand why Mr. Cibber should want to saddle himself with a woman like me. Besides, you know as well as I do that the Marquis of Troon who is my Guardian will send the Police to find me, and that might prove very dangerous for all of you."

"Th' Markiss o' Troon," the man repeated, pronouncing the words wrong. " 'E be the bruvver, of Mr. Stev . . . !"

He stopped as if he realised he was being indiscreet, but Valeta was well aware of what he had been about to say.

Was Lionel Stevington involved in this? she asked herself.

She had heard her father relate often enough the disgraceful way he was behaving in London.

Their friends who genuinely worked to try to relieve some of the wide-spread suffering of the poor, always spoke of Lionel Stevington with contempt. They knew he did nothing really to help the people he professed to champion, but merely incited them to violence for his own ends.

"I think the old Marquis would turn in his grave," Sir Charles had said more than once, "if he knew how his younger son was behaving."

On one occasion Valeta knew he had discussed Lionel Stevington with the Bishop of London who had taken the place of her grandfather after he died.

"The Bishop says that Lionel Stevington is appealing to the young ne'er-do-wells, and sooner or later," Sir Charles had said, "he will cause a riot which will have to be crushed by the Military."

"Oh, I hope not!" Valeta had exclaimed.

She had been upset more than once by hearing of the riots that had taken place in London and various other parts of the country and which had been put down in an almost brutal manner.

This year, when the Regent had opened Parliament in January, he had driven through a very hostile crowd. Gravel and stones were thrown at the Royal carriage and some windows were broken.

The result of this had been that the Habeas Corpus Act was suspended, which meant that anybody under suspicion of causing trouble could be thrown into gaol and kept there.

Both Sir Charles and Valeta thought that in such circumstances quite a number of innocent people might be arrested when they had been doing nothing more sinister than walking peacefully about the streets.

Once in prison they had little chance of getting out unless somebody with influence interceded on their behalf.

Magistrates everywhere in the country had the power to send to gaol any person they thought likely to commit an act prejudicial to public order before they had even done so.

Sir Charles heard of cases where obstreperous boys pulling a face, or making a rude noise, had been shut away behind bars.

The terrifying thing was that there was nothing the ordinary citizen could do against this injustice.

It was no use trying to march to Westminster to present a petition against this abuse of power, because there was an Act prohibiting meetings of more than fifty persons within a mile of Westminster Hall.

Severe punishments for the slightest offence continued to be given simply because the real truth was the Government was frightened of revolutionaries.

So in the circumstances it seemed extraordinary to Valeta that an uneducated Sweep like Cibber, foul though he might be in his speech and cruel to his apprentices, would think of committing the outrageous crime of abducting a lady.

"Unless of course," she told herself, "he has been instigated by somebody of a very different class, and that person might easily be Lionel Stevington!"

But why? Why should Lionel Stevington be concerned with her when as far as she knew, he had never even seen her, much less spoken to her?

She herself had sometimes seen him riding through the Park when he was younger and living at home, and on several occasions recently when he had called to see his brother and left without staying the night.

From the Manor House it was possible to see the carriages passing down the drive, and as Valeta regularly used to walk in the Park for exercise she often had a good view of visitors on their way to or from the great house.

Lionel Stevington was, she thought, something like the Marquis in looks, but while she felt contemptuous of the Marquis for his rakish behaviour, he did not disgust or frighten her as a man.

Lionel Stevington did both, and she knew instinctively as he passed her with his grim, un-smiling face, that he was bad.

She thought she would make sure of her suspicions and after a moment she asked:

"Where am I meeting Mr. Stevington?"

" 'E said . . ." the man opposite began, then broke off to shout angrily:

"Will ye stop askin' questions. Oi h'ain't tellin' yer nothin'. D'yer und'stand?"

"I understand," Valeta said quietly, but she had learned what she wanted to know.

She busied herself talking to Harry and pulling him a little nearer for comfort, and put her arm around him.

He was a sturdy little boy and she thought once again how thankful she was that he was not Nicholas, sensitive and highly strung, who would have been in an abject state of terror if he were with her now.

They drove on and although Valeta made various efforts to converse with the man opposite, he made no response.

In fact she realised she was frightening him by her questions when he said:

"If yer go on talkin' Oi'll make yer cover yersel' up again. D'yer 'ear?""

"Yes, I hear," Valeta said.

Fearing he might put his threat into execution, she did not address him again, but talked only to Harry.

"Me Pa will be angry when I don't go home," the boy said.

"I am sure he will be, and he will come to look for you," Valeta replied. "Then Nicholas will tell him who has taken you away."

She saw by the look in the man's eyes listening that this possibility had not occurred to him.

"I suppose," she told herself, "that man Cibber thought he could just snatch Nicholas and me away, and nobody would know where we had gone. But now Nicholas will perhaps have recognised one of these men."

On the other hand there was always the chance that Nicholas intent on playing with his toys, had not paid any attention to what was going on outside.

But Nanny, Valeta thought, would find some way of letting the Marquis know what had occurred.

Then she remembered with a sudden leap of her heart that he was calling for her at eleven o'clock to take her to luncheon with his mother.

She had actually forgotten about it until this moment because being carried off in such a frightening fashion had put everything else out of her mind.

Now she remembered the Marquis would call and Nanny would tell him what had happened.

She felt the warm glow of relief flood over her and the fear that had been like a sharp dagger in her breast, although she tried to control it, receded a little.

What was the time now? she wondered. Not more than perhaps nine-thirty, but in an hour-

and-a-half the Marquis would call at the Manor and learn that she had been abducted in this extraordinary manner.

It was such a comfort to know that he would soon learn of her terrible plight that she said to Harry:

"You need not be frightened. These wicked men will get their just desserts and perhaps sooner than they expect!"

"An' yer'll get wot's comin' to yer!" the man opposite her retorted.

"At least I shall not be transported across the sea," Valeta answered. "I understand the ships in which the convicts are chained are very uncomfortable and many of the prisoners die of starvation."

"Shut yer mouf, or Oi'll shut it for yer!" the man shouted angrily.

"I am sorry," Valeta said, "I am very sorry for you."

He looked over his shoulder as if somehow he wished to communicate with his friends on the box outside, but he made no effort to attract their attention and Valeta thought there would be nothing he could do until they reached their destination.

It seemed to take hours for the carriage to reach the outskirts of the city, and then begin to make its way through narrow and crowded streets which were rougher and more poverty-stricken than any Valeta had ever seen before.

Her father had described to her so often the

horrors of the London slums and the misery of the inhabitants who were forced to live there.

It suddenly struck her that Cibber with his filthy sacks of soot and the miserable half-starved children he employed in his trade, might live in St. Giles'.

She had read and heard of the horrors that existed in a part of London which should have been swept away, Sir Charles always said, a hundred years ago.

It was there, Valeta knew, that the maimed and the blind beggars, the women with sick bare-footed children (hired for the day), and soldiers and sailors with bogus wounds congregated.

"It is a camp," Sir Charles had said once, "for the lowest type of vagrant, the petty thief, and those who have sunk too low to be fit for even the roughest company elsewhere."

"My father has told me," Lady Lingfield said in her soft voice, "that they fill the old houses from garret to cellar, six or seven to a room, and the streets into which no light, let alone the sun, can percolate reek with the piles of decaying litter and all manner of offal."

"Something must be done about it," Sir Charles said firmly.

He went on saying the same thing after Valeta's mother was dead and he still tried to get organisations to help the pregnant women and save some of the children from becoming criminals from the very moment they could walk.

Valeta remembered learning some of the

houses in St. Giles' had 'schools' for the criminal training of the young.

Both girls and boys were taught the 'kinchin-lay' 'clyfaking', 'wipe-snitching,' and how to 'nim a ticker', and were sent out to work amongst the crowds.

"My father has often told me that when he was young and worked in those terrible streets," Lady Lingfield related, "above the nightly racket could always be heard screams of those who had come home empty-handed and were being beaten for it."

Valeta did not know why, but she was quite certain that was where she and Harry were being taken.

St. Giles'!

The area which made even the strongest young men in the priesthood draw in their breath, and which was a by-word for everything that was criminal and lawless.

She found herself praying that somehow the Marquis would save her, and yet how would he guess for one moment that his brother was involved in anything so reprehensible as a kidnapping?

If it was a question of a ransom, she supposed that sooner or later Lionel Stevington would get in touch with his brother.

She had known he was always hard up for money because that was an open secret amongst the employees on the Troon estate.

"Master Lionel be here again," she had heard

one man say when he did not know she was listening. "I expects he's come to 'nick' anything he can't persuade His Lordship to give him, 'a sharpster', they tell is what he be called in London!"

It was not the way that anyone should speak of the Stevington family, Valeta had thought severely.

At the same time, how could those who had served the great house all their lives be expected to have any respect for Lionel when they learned of his revolutionary speeches and the manner in which he abused his brother and his own class in public?

The streets in which they were driving grew narrower and narrower and now Valeta knew with all certainty that they were in St. Giles'.

She could see the flaring lights of the gin shops at every corner, and she could see too the filthy drains running through the centre of the streets in which half-naked children with bare feet were playing.

She began to grow more and more apprehensive.

The people she could see through the windows of the carriage all seemed to have grotesque faces, many of them distorted by disease or debauched by drink.

At last the horses turned into a small yard and now Valeta knew they had reached their destination, for the yard was piled with sacks of soot.

The horses came to a standstill and the man

who had been with them inside the carriage opened the door and jumped out.

She heard him telling the two men descending from the box that they had brought the wrong boy.

"It be th' wrong lad we 'ave 'ere. Nichilas be left a'ind. The woman says," pointing his finger at Valeta as she still sat inside the carriage, "that 'e'll tell as where 'em two 'as been took."

Valeta could not see clearly the faces of the two men who had been on the box, but she had a feeling they were shocked by the information.

Then the one who had been driving and was obviously an older man said:

"Put 'em two inside an' let's see wat Cibber 'as t' say abaht it."

The man who had been with them in the carriage came to the door.

"Aht yer git," he said, "an' sharp 'bout it!"

Valeta stepped out first, holding up her skirts as she followed the man who was walking ahead of them into the house.

The yard was filthy and there was the smell of soot and other things to which she had no wish to put a name.

The room they entered opened onto the street on the opposite side and was furnished with a rusty stove, a deal table and several hard-chairs, most of which had some part of them broken.

The walls were dark with dirt and smoke and what windows there were had their broken panes stuffed with rags so that it was almost impossible to see.

When Valeta would have stopped the man ahead beckoned to her and she was led round a corner into another room which was even more unprepossessing than the first.

Here, as in the yard, there was nothing but sacks of soot, many of them spilling out their contents.

There were no chairs, nothing on which to sit but the sacks which Valeta realised would make her black even to touch them.

She was about to ask a question of the man who led them there, but he was already moving out through the door and pulling it behind him.

"Wait a moment!" Valeta called. But he was gone and she heard him thrust home a bolt.

"Why have — those men brought us — here?" Harry asked in a frightened voice.

"I do not know," Valeta replied.

Then she put her fingers to her lips and moved a little nearer the door as she realised that she could overhear what the men were saying in the next room.

The door, while it kept them prisoner, was ill-fitting and several wooden panels were cracked so that the voices were very clear.

She heard the men quarrelling amongst themselves because they had brought the wrong boy.

" 'Ow was Oi ter know it weren't young Nichilas?" one man asked in an aggrieved tone. " 'E's got fair 'air, ain't 'e? 'E was wi' th' snazzy doll."

Valeta realised this was a reference to herself.

166

"Cibber won't loik it," one man said. "Nor 'is Nibs. 'E said over and over again that once they were 'ere nobody'd know where they'd gorn."

"Us'll 'ave to tell 'im."

"Ye can do that, seein' as 'ow yer picked oop th' boy."

" 'Ow was Oi ter know? 'Is 'air's th' same as Nichilas an' 'e's abaht th' same size."

"No, 'e ain't."

Valeta recognised the voice of the man who had been in the carriage with them.

" 'E won't get oop 'em smaller chimleys — Oi can tell yer that!"

Valeta drew in her breath.

As she had suspected, they intended to use Nicholas again as a climbing boy, and although she was glad he was safe from the horror of it, she could not bear to think of Harry's suffering when they subjected him to the torture of being forced up a chimney.

Where was the Marquis?

Surely, she thought, by now he must have learned what had occurred and be on his way to London?

Then, insidiously, the question came as to whether he would be interested. He had not wanted her for his Ward. Why should he put himself out now?

Perhaps he would send a servant, or Mr. Chamberlain, and she had a feeling that the latter might easily be hoodwinked by these ruffians while the Marquis would know them for what they were.

He had been so brave and so gallant in the war. He would not be afraid whatever the numbers against him.

"He will find us," Valeta said reassuringly to herself. "I know he will!"

Harry was holding tightly to her hand and she was just going to say something comforting to him when she heard the men in the next room say apprehensively:

" 'Ere 'e comes!"

There was the sound of heavy footsteps, then a loud aggressive voice that Valeta recognised as belonging to Cibber the Sweep.

" 'Ere yer be!" he said, shouting rather than speaking. "Oi meant ter be 'ere to meet yer, but Oi gets 'eld up. Th' blasted boy got stuck in a chimley an' half-suffocated, 'e were. But 'e'll recover."

Cibber must have walked into the centre of the room and when the three men did not speak, he said:

"Well? Wot've yer got ter tell me? 'Ave yer got 'em 'ere?"

"Yes, they're 'ere, in the next room."

"Well, that's satisfactory, that is! Th' Guvnor'll be 'ere in a second or two, an' yer'll get yer money."

"Jus' one fing went wrong."

"Wrong?" Cibber asked. "Wot d'yer mean — wrong?"

168

"We ain't got Nichilas."

"Yer ain't got Nichilas? Why not?"

"Us picks up anuvver boy by mistike."

"Mistake?"

Cibber roared the word and it seemed to echo and re-echo. Because it was so loud Harry gave a little murmur of fear and moved closer to Valeta.

It was then that Valeta heard another voice, educated and yet somehow in its very manner sounding unpleasant.

"Here you all are! I gather from the fact that the carriage outside is empty, that our plunder is in the next room?"

"Yus, Guv'nor, in th' next room. Jus' like yer wanted em."

"The woman and the boy?"

"Yus, Guv — excep' . . ."

"Except what?"

The question was sharp.

"Us were jus' tellin' Mr. Cibber 'ere there's been a bit o' a mistike. Us brung th' wrong boy."

"You mean you left the boy Nicholas behind?"

"Yus, Guv, 'twas by haccident, so ter speak."

"That was an incredibly stupid thing to do."

Lionel Stevington's voice was sharp and biting as a whip.

" 'Twas a mistake, Guv, but us brung th' woman, jus' as yer said."

"I will deal with her, but I suppose you are aware that Nicholas will give us away if he recognised any of you?"

169

"Us never seed 'im, Guv'nor. Don't fink 'e were there."

"You are sure? Quite sure you didn't see him?"

"Nah, Guv. Not sight nor sound o' 'im."

Valeta realised that Lionel Stevington was thinking hard and wondering if he should believe them.

Then one of the men said:

"If us can 'ave our Jimmy o' gobbins, Guv, us'll be gettin' along."

"Very well. I suppose you did your best. It is extraordinary how there are always mistakes unless I do everything myself!"

There was no answer to this but there was the clink of coins, a low mutter which might have been gratitude, then the sound of the men's feet moving away.

"Damned fools!" Lionel Stevington exclaimed. "Why the devil could they not have brought the right child?"

" 'Tis ool right if Nichilas didn't see Bill."

"Can we believe them when they said there was no sign of the boy?"

"Oi 'opes so," Cibber said, "but t' make sure, Oi'll push this new boy off onto one o' me mates. Oi don' wanna be found wiv 'im on me 'ands, so t' speak."

"Yes, that would be the wise thing to do," Lionel Stevington agreed. "Then if you are short-handed it might be possible to get hold of the other boy again."

"Too dangerous!" Cibber said. "Oi don't like

170

takin' risks, an' that makes Oi hask: 'Wot abaht th' woman?' "

"You need not worry about her," Lionel Stevington said. "Old Mother Baggott will be along very shortly and after that we shall hear no more of her."

"Be that safe?" Cibber asked. " 'Er'll talk."

"Not when Baggott's given her the juice of the poppy."

Cibber laughed an ugly rough sound.

"Oi'd always 'eard that 'as 'ow she works."

"It keeps them pliable for the first weeks until they are hooked on it. Then they have no wish to escape."

Valeta drew in her breath.

Any other girl of her age brought up in different circumstances might not have understood, but her father and mother had talked openly of the horrors that went on in London.

She was well aware that the procurers of young girls kept them either in a state of intoxication, or doped with opium until they were too bemused to know what they were doing.

She felt that what was being said could only be happening in a bad dream, and yet in a terrifying manner the words made sense and she could be in no doubt as to what lay in front of her.

She resisted an impulse to scream and beat her hands against the bolted door, but she knew that to do so would only attract attention and she would perhaps be made unconscious even sooner than was planned.

It seemed incredible that Lionel Stevington who had been born a gentleman should behave in such a manner, and yet now every tale, every innuendo in someone's voice, every disapproving look, came back to tell her that he was even worse than she had suspected.

How, she wondered, could she have hated the Marquis or found fault with his behaviour when his brother Lionel to all intents and purposes, was as wicked as the devil himself?

She was trembling and because he knew she was afraid Harry began to tremble too.

"What are we agoing to do, Miss?" he whispered, and Valeta could not find words or a voice in which to answer him.

She could only shut her eyes and pray weakly that if the Marquis did not arrive to save her she might die before the woman who was to take her into a bawdy house arrived.

Then she heard Cibber say:

"Oi thinks, Guv, Oi'd best be gettin' along wi' th' boy. No point in hangin' abaht."

"No, off you go, Cibber. I will wait here for Mother Baggott. She will not let me down, and it will certainly be to her advantage not to do so."

There was an evil undertone in Lionel's voice, as though he was positively enjoying the idea of Valeta being handed over to such a woman.

Cibber must have turned towards the bolted door, for Valeta heard his footsteps coming towards them.

Instinctively she recoiled, pulling Harry by the hand.

There was very little room to move because of the sacks on the floor, and just as Cibber must have raised his hand to the bolt, there was the sound of a voice saying in a tone of authority:

"Is there a man called Cibber here?"

Valeta gave a little cry, but it could hardly pass her lips. Then she felt her heart leap and begin to beat frantically, for she knew that the Marquis had arrived and was outside in the court-yard.

Cibber walked back to the other room as the Marquis was saying:

"What a surprise, Lionel, to find you here, but I might have expected it!"

"What do you want?" Lionel Stevington asked angrily. "Is not Troon enough for you that you have to come bursting into my part of the world?"

"If you consider this stinking place a possession of yours, then you are welcome to it," the Marquis replied, "but I understand that you and your hired felons have stolen something which belongs to me."

"And what can that be?" Lionel asked.

"There is no need to keep up any pretence," the Marquis replied, "although I am still somewhat at sea to understand why my Ward should be of interest to you."

"I have no idea what you are talking about," Lionel Stevington protested.

"Then let me put it into words of one syllable," the Marquis said. "Cibber, who shall be taken before the Magistrates for this, has kidnapped the son of one of my farmers and he well knows the penalty."

"Oi didn't do nuffin' o' th' sort!" Cibber shouted in his usual manner. "Mr. Stevin'ton 'ere tells Oi 'e wants the boy brung t' London. Oi wasn't takin' 'im back in th' trade — not a'ter yer'd bought 'im from me, M'Lord. Nuffin' crooked abaht me!"

"You can say that at your trial," the Marquis said bluntly. "But what is your excuse, Lionel, for abducting a young girl who happens to be my Ward?"

"I have told you I do not know what you are talking about," Lionel Stevington repeated, "and you will find it very hard to prove your accusation."

Although she was certain that the Marquis would not be deceived by such blatant lies, Valeta could take no chances.

She beat on the door, calling out:

"We are here! We are here! Save us!"

The Marquis smiled.

"That sounds like pretty conclusive proof to me, Lionel. Now suppose you get out of my way and let me release my Ward and my farmer's son before I teach you a lesson which you will not forget in a hurry!"

As the Marquis spoke he told himself that while Lionel and Cibber might put up a fight, he and Freddie had them pretty well matched.

Granted Cibber was a huge, strong, beefy

man, but the Marquis was quite certain he had only an elementary knowledge of boxing while he and Freddie were both pupils of "Gentleman Jackson's Salon" in Bond Street.

There were few of their friends who could beat them when it came to a fight.

At this moment it had not entered the Marquis's mind for one moment that he carried a loaded pistol and that Freddie who was standing just inside the doorway of the dirty room and who had not joined in the conversation, had another.

He was quite prepared to fight it out man to man and in fact, the idea was a pleasure.

This was the opportunity for which he had waited a long time, to give Lionel the thrashing he thoroughly deserved with no unfair advantage to either of them except that the premises in which they had to fight were somewhat restricting.

Then as he looked at his brother with a faint smile on his lips, knowing that Lionel was loathing him with the fanatical, unnatural hatred which he had shown ever since they had been children together, Lionel pulled a pistol from his pocket.

"Not so fast!" he said furiously. "If you are not out of here within three seconds, Serle, I will shoot you and Freddie down where you stand!"

"Do not be a fool, Lionel!" the Marquis said. "However much you dislike me, I am not worth swinging for."

"I will not do that," Lionel replied. "I shall be tried by my Peers and if there is an enquiry, Cibber here will swear on oath that you attacked me first."

"I think you must be crazy!" the Marquis said. "Come on, Lionel. I have prevented you from committing a quite unnecessary crime, so be a sport and allow me to release Miss Lingfield and the small boy who is not climbing anybody's chimneys, and take them back to Troon."

The Marquis spoke in a conciliatory tone, but at the same time, his eyes were wary.

He saw an expression on Lionel's face that he had seen once or twice before and which he had told himself then, as he did now, was undoubtedly a look of madness.

He had, in fact, thought for several years, that his brother was becoming steadily insane and when he had mentioned his suspicions to the family Physician, the old man who had known the Stevington boys all their lives, had said:

"I've had a feeling for some time that your brother Lionel has something dangerously wrong with him. It may be an affliction of the brain, for the tantrums he indulged in as a child have obviously increased and he should be having medical treatment."

"I doubt if I could persuade him to do that," the Marquis replied, "even though I am prepared to pay for it."

The old Doctor shook his head and said

nothing, but every time the Marquis saw his brother after that he was certain that the diagnosis had been correct.

Therefore he chose his words and spoke in a conciliatory manner which made Freddie look at him in surprise.

"Come on, Lionel," he said. "Stop pointing that unpleasant weapon at me, and let us have a laugh about this childish prank. I know as well as you do that you did not intend it to be serious."

"It is damned serious to me," Lionel said fiercely through clenched teeth. "How do you think I felt when that woman on whom you have been lavishing the family fortune told me you were going to marry a girl?"

His voice seemed to rise higher as he cried:

"Marry, and do me out of my inheritance? You will not have a son, if I can help it!"

He fired his pistol as he spoke, but the Marquis, who had seen his finger tighten on the trigger, flung himself on the floor a split second before the bullet crashed into the wall behind him, dislodging a large lump of dirty plaster.

The explosion from Lionel's pistol was followed almost instantaneously by another.

For a moment it seemed as if Lionel had not been hit. Then he fell slowly and almost ludicrously onto the dirty floor.

Cibber gave a shout of terror and stumbling over the fallen body ran from the house and across the yard to disappear into the crowds on the streets outside.

The Marquis picked himself up slowly.

"Is he dead?" he asked.

Freddie stepped forward to look down at Lionel who was now lying on his back, the blood seeping slowly over his shirt-front from a bullet hole just above his heart.

"I thought he had killed you!"

"I realised just in time that was what he intended to do," the Marquis replied.

He pulled the lapels of his riding-coat into place, walked across the room and pulled back the bolt on the door.

As it opened Valeta, frantic with fear, deafened by the sound of the pistol shots and unable to hear what had followed them, stood looking at him, her face as white as her gown.

Then she gave a little cry and moved swiftly towards him.

Neither was certain how it happened, but the Marquis's arms were round her and she was trembling against him, her face hidden against his shoulder.

"It is all right," he said. "You are safe!"

CHAPTER SEVEN

Valeta did not move, but it seemed to the Marquis as if she was clinging to him as tightly as Nicholas had done.

Instinctively he held her closer as he said:

"It is really all right, and you need no longer be afraid."

"You . . . are not . . . hurt?"

He could hardly hear her voice, it was so low, and she was still trembling, although not so violently.

"I am unhurt," he said. "So let us get out of this ghastly place!"

He turned round to face the door, but kept his arm round her shoulder.

Somehow they managed to walk through it together and Harry followed them. Then just before they turned the corner into the next room the Marquis stopped.

"I want you to shut your eyes," he said. "I am going to carry you out into the yard."

Valeta did not speak, but he knew instinctively that she was asking why.

"There is something I do not want you to see," he explained.

As if she understood what it was, she said faintly:

"Harry?"

"Yes, of course," the Marquis replied, as if he

remembered the child for the first time.

"Listen Harry," he said to the child behind them, "I want you to wait here until I come back for you. You are not to move, you are not to go any further. Do you understand?"

"Yes, M'Lord," Harry said obediently.

His face was streaked with tears, but he appeared to be no longer afraid and the Marquis liked the firm manner in which he spoke.

"That is a good boy," he approved. "Now wait until I come back."

He picked Valeta up in his arms as he spoke.

"Shut your eyes," he ordered, "and do not open them until I tell you you can."

She did as he told her and turned her face against his shoulder. He had the idea that she was feeling too limp to do anything but what she was told to do.

Freddie must have heard what the Marquis said, for he walked ahead of them into the yard and opened the carriage door which was standing where the men had left it, the horses unattended but too spiritless to move.

The Marquis set Valeta down on the back seat. As he did so she opened her eyes.

His face was very near to hers and for a moment they looked at each other without moving. Then almost abruptly the Marquis said:

"I will fetch Harry. Stay where you are and do not look out of the window."

He walked away and Valeta with a little gasp, leant back in the corner of the carriage.

She could hardly believe that what had taken place was not part of her imagination. Yet the Marquis had come and rescued her as she had prayed he might do, and now, as he had said, there was no need to be afraid.

But the horror she had felt when she listened to Lionel Stevington was still there like an evil shadow, and she felt as if her whole body was shrinking from a fate that was so terrifying that even now she trembled at the thought of it.

"He has . . . saved me!" she whispered to herself and heard the Marquis coming back with Harry in his arms.

"Now you can open your eyes, my boy," he said, "and do not be a nuisance to Miss Lingfield."

He turned back and Harry asked in a bewildered tone:

"What's agoing to — happen to us now — Miss?"

Because she knew the child was bemused by everything that had occurred, Valeta forced herself to say quietly:

"It is quite all right. The Marquis will take us home and you will be with your father and mother again."

Harry seemed to find this idea satisfactory, and Valeta closed her eyes fighting against a sudden faintness that seemed to seep over her like a mist rising over the water.

"I must be sensible," she thought, "it is all over, and I cannot be so weak and foolish as to swoon . . ."

But she felt herself drifting away into uncon-sciousness . . .

The next thing Valeta heard was the Marquis's voice saying:

"Have you a flask with you, Freddie?"

"There is not much in it," Freddie remarked. "I needed a drink myself after what happened just now."

"It will be enough," the Marquis said.

Valeta felt his arm behind her head, then something hard against her lips.

"Drink this!" the Marquis said firmly and be-cause she had no will to oppose him, she did as he said.

She felt something fiery searing her throat and put up her hand in protest.

"Just another sip," the Marquis said, and be-cause she could not argue with him, she did as she was told.

"I am . . . sorry," she tried to say as he took the silver cup from her lips.

Then unaccountably she had an almost un-controllable desire to hide her face against him and burst into tears.

But with an almost superhuman effort she made herself say a little unsteadily:

"I . . . am . . . all right."

"I tell you what we will do, Freddie," the Mar-quis said, "we will drive this ramshackle old box to where we left the Phaeton. I am not allowing Valeta to walk through these filthy streets."

"A good idea!" Freddie agreed. "Shall I drive, or will you?"

"You drive," the Marquis replied, "if you think you are capable of making these tortoises move!"

"Can I — help, Sir?" Harry asked brightening up at the thought of going home.

"Come on then," Freddie said good-humouredly, "although whether we can turn the horses round in this hole I have not the slightest idea!"

He shut the carriage door and climbed up on the box with Harry following him.

The Marquis and Valeta were left alone.

He had not taken his arm from around her and his face was very near to hers.

As if she felt she must say something, if only to alleviate her shyness, she said:

"Thank . . . you for . . . saving us. I was . . . praying that . . . you would."

"It was fortunate that Nicholas recognised Bill, whoever that might be," the Marquis said.

"I . . . hoped he might . . . recognise somebody . . . but if . . . you had not . . . come . . ."

She shivered as she remembered the fate that Lionel had planned for her.

"Forget it," the Marquis said. "My brother, as I expect you realise, is dead."

"Did you . . . shoot him?"

"No, Freddie did when he tried to kill me."

"Supposing . . . just supposing he had . . . succeeded?"

"Would that have worried you?" the Marquis asked.

"He was . . . sending me to . . . a bawdy . . . house."

He could hardly hear the words. Then because even to think of it was so appalling, Valeta instinctively hid her face against the Marquis's shoulder.

She knew that for a moment he was tense with anger, then he said:

"My brother was mad. It is the only explanation I can give for his behaviour."

The carriage began to rock as with some difficulty and by moving the horses backwards and forwards Freddie turned round in the sack-filled yard.

The Marquis held Valeta closer and more firmly. Soon they were out in the narrow street, hearing the shouts of the children and the jeers of harridans propping up the doorways of their dirty houses, holding out the goods from their old clothes shops or handling food which was already in a state of stinking decay.

Freddie drove expertly with small boys running beside the carriage and ragged members of the populace shrieking abuse as the wheels threw up the filthy drain water from the gutter.

Then in a very short time they had moved into a wider and quieter street where the Phaeton was waiting for them.

Freddie drew the horses to a standstill and jumping down from the box, opened the door.

"What am I to do with this old Ark?" he asked, as the Marquis got out and turned to help Valeta.

"Send a boy to take it back to where it belongs," the Marquis replied. "I have no desire to be accused of being a horse-stealer on top of everything else!"

"A good idea!" Freddie agreed.

One of the bigger boys who had followed the carriage was gaping at them as they talked. Freddie beckoned him.

"You look an honest lad," he said. "If I pay you, will you lead these horses, and I mean lead — not drive them — back to Cibber's yard?"

The boy's eyes brightened.

"Yer'll pay Oi, Guv'nor?"

"I will certainly pay you," Freddie said, "but you have to promise me that you will deliver them safely and while you are about it, give the animals something to eat and drink."

"Orl roight, Guv'nor."

"Very well, I trust you," Freddie said, "and if you do not do as I tell you, I think you will find that Mr. Cibber will have something to say to you!"

He knew by the expression on the youth's face that this was quite a powerful threat.

Freddie handed him several silver coins which made him gasp with delight before he stowed them swiftly away in some obscure part of his ragged clothing from which there was no likelihood of their being pinched.

Then he walked away, leading the horses as he had been told.

The Marquis had already helped Valeta into the Phaeton.

"I will tell you what we will do first," he said. "We will go to Stevington House and have something to eat. Then I think, Freddie, you had better call on the Home Secretary and tell him that Lionel is dead."

"That is just what I was thinking myself," Freddie said. "As it happens, he is a friend of my father's so there is every likelihood he will believe me when I tell him the truth."

"It seems unkind," the Marquis said, "but I have a feeling that nobody will mourn Lionel and that those in high places who have resented his behaviour will actually rejoice!"

"Are you going to leave him where he is?" Freddie asked.

The two men had both been speaking in low voices so that Valeta should not hear what they said.

"No, of course not," the Marquis answered. "When I get to Stevington House I will make arrangements for his body to be collected and taken to Troon where he will be buried with due ceremony in the family vault."

"It is certainly more than he deserves," Freddie said. "It might have been you who were taken there in his place."

"I will express my gratitude on a more suitable occasion," the Marquis said, "but as it happens we are now even."

Freddie smiled for the first time since the conversation had begun.

"I have not forgotten that you saved my life at Waterloo."

"Nor have I," the Marquis replied. "I was wondering when you would repay the debt."

Freddie laughed and the Marquis swung himself up into the seat on the Phaeton.

"You can squeeze in beside Valeta," he said. "The boy on the floor. It will be a little cramped, but I will get you made into a more Savoy neighbourhood as quickly as I can."

The groom sprang away from the horses' heads and jumped up behind and they drove off, Valeta squeezed between the Marquis and Freddie, thinking that their close proximity made her feel safe in a manner that was curiously comforting.

Only when they reached the more fashionable streets did she suddenly become self-conscious, aware that she was wearing no bonnet and her hair after being covered by the cloth, was doubtless untidy.

She put up her hands to her head and the Marquis, as if he was aware of what she was thinking, said:

"Do not worry. You look very lovely."

The compliment was so unexpected that for a moment she stared at him wide-eyed.

"You are very brave," the Marquis said. "Most women having been through what you have, would be having hysterics."

"Of course they would," Freddie agreed, "and with reason. A more filthy, horrible place than that Sweep's house I could not imagine in a thousand years. Something ought to be done about it, and the whole of St. Giles'."

"I agree," the Marquis said, "and what is more, I am determined that something shall be done!"

Valeta who had turned her head towards Freddie when he spoke now looked back at the Marquis.

"Do you really . . . mean that?" she asked.

"I mean it," the Marquis confirmed. "The whole place should be demolished and burned to the ground, and the people who live there given the chance of a better sort of life."

Valeta clasped her hands together.

"If only Papa and Mama could hear you," she said. "It was what they always prayed would happen. Other parts of London are bad, but St. Giles' is the worst of the lot!"

"Something will have to be done!" the Marquis said determinedly.

And again inexplicably Valeta felt she was going to cry.

She was sure however, that both the Marquis and Freddie would despise her if she did so. So she bit her lip and blinked her eye-lashes forcing the tears away, but for some moments she was unable to speak.

By now they had moved swiftly into the wider

streets of Mayfair and were only a short distance from Park Lane.

They drew up at the front door of Stevington House and when the servants in the magnificent livery hurriedly appeared to lay down red carpet, once again Valeta became conscious of her appearance.

The Marquis however, was already inside the Hall before Freddie could help Valeta from the Phaeton.

"I want luncheon to be served as quickly as possible," he said, "and ask the Housekeeper to attend to Miss Lingfield."

Then as Harry appeared he said to the Butler:

"Look after the small boy. He comes from Troon. Feed him, and I shall be taking him back with me this afternoon."

"Very good, M'Lord."

The Butler appeared to be quite used to receiving strange orders and in a few minutes a footman led Valeta upstairs to where the Housekeeper was waiting for her on the landing.

"If you will come this way, Miss," she said respectfully.

Rustling in her black silk dress she walked ahead to lead Valeta into a large and attractive bedroom.

"You must think it very strange," Valeta said, "that I have no bonnet, but . . ."

She was right in thinking that the Housekeeper was curious and she explained a little lamely that she had come to London at a moment's notice without time even to put on a travelling gown and pick up her bonnet and gloves.

She was quite certain that sooner or later the gossip about what had actually occurred would percolate from Troon, to Stevington House, but she had no desire at the moment to relate to anybody the terrible experience through which she had passed.

"Don't you worry, Miss," the Housekeeper said. "If you are returning to Troon with His Lordship this afternoon I'm sure I can find you something to wear, although it might not be in the very latest fashion."

"I shall be glad of anything," Valeta said. "I am afraid I would feel very untidy if I travelled in His Lordship's Phaeton without a bonnet."

"Leave everything to me, Miss," the Housekeeper said.

With her hair tidy, her face and hands washed, and several marks of soot sponged from her gown, Valeta went down the stairs a little while later feeling somewhat self-conscious.

In the magnificent house the Marquis was back in her mind as the authoritative, unapproachable Guardian she had thought him to be when she was at home.

It was embarrassing to remember how she had thrown herself into his arms when he had opened the door in the Sweep's house and how she had hidden her face against him in the carriage.

"Perhaps he will be shocked that I was so forward," she told herself and blushed at what she imagined might be his condemnation of her behaviour.

Then she knew however much she surprised or even shocked him she could never be grateful enough for that moment when with the shots ringing in her ears and in terror at what might be occurring, she had seen him standing in the doorway.

At that moment he had been all the heroes of her childhood rolled into one: Sir Galahad, St. George and Perseus and certainly no longer the man she hated.

"Now he will save not only me but thousands of other people, if he keeps to what he said," she told herself.

Because she was so excited at the thought she felt as if her feet had wings as they carried her down the stairs.

She had a sudden urgency to see the Marquis so that he could confirm what he had said and she could really believe there was hope for all the people whom her mother had worried over and whose plight had often made her father swear beneath his breath.

In the Salon, a glass of champagne in his hand, the Marquis was saying to Freddie:

"I have already sent to collect Lionel's body, and I have told them to notify the Magistrates and the Bow Street Police on the way, so that they can see the position of the body and that Lionel has a pistol in his hand that has been fired."

"I will explain it all when I get to the Home

Office," Freddie promised.

"I am hoping you can arrange for neither of our names to be brought into it," the Marquis said. "I have a feeling they will not like the fact that the incident took place in St. Giles'."

"What makes you say that?"

"Because if they are not ashamed of the damned place they ought to be!" the Marquis said sharply.

The way he spoke made his friend turn and look at him with raised eye-brows.

"I seem to recognise that tone of voice! It is the one you used to use when you had seen the atrocities the French committed and you decided to have your revenge on them."

"That is exactly how I am feeling now," the Marquis said.

"If you are thinking of fighting such conditions," Freddie said half-jokingly, "it will take you a long time before you achieve a victory."

"It will certainly keep me busy," the Marquis said.

Freddie looked at him speculatively for a moment, then put down his champagne glass.

"I always rather fancied you as a Crusader, Serle," he said, "and with Dilys out of the way and no longer offering you all the temptations of Eve, you might even find it an interesting occupation."

"That is just what I was thinking myself," the Marquis said quietly.

"Perhaps after all, though it is infuriating to

think so, Dilys has done you a good turn," Freddie said.

"It will certainly be the first and the last," the Marquis said firmly.

As he spoke the door opened and Valeta came in.

Valeta awoke with a feeling that something strange had happened, but she was not quite certain what it was.

Then she opened her eyes and remembered.

She was at Troon, sleeping in a room that was ten times the size of her bedroom at the Manor and she could see the sunshine percolating through the sides of the curtains, picking out the gold cupids that climbed the posts of the great bed in which she was lying.

It had been late in the afternoon yesterday when they had arrived back at Troon to find Nanny frantic with anxiety and Nicholas overjoyed to see her.

As the Marquis drew up his horses outside the front door Nicholas who, Valeta learned later, had insisted on staying at one of the windows on the first floor all the afternoon waiting for her and watching the drive, had come tearing down the stairs to fling himself into her arms.

"You are back! You are back!" he cried. "Nanny said His Lordship would rescue you, but I was afraid, terribly afraid you were lost."

"I am not lost, dearest," Valeta said, holding him very tight.

A moment later Nanny's arms were round her and the old woman was shedding tears of thankfulness.

"It is not like you, Nanny, to cry," Valeta said.

"I'm getting old, that's what's the matter with me," Nanny said stoutly, "and I can't stand these shocks."

"It is all over," Valeta said comfortingly, "and His Lordship saved us both."

She saw as she spoke Nicholas run to the Marquis with a cry of joy, and to her surprise he bent down to pick the child up in his arms.

"You brought her back!" Nicholas exclaimed. "I knew you would. I knew it! Nanny cried and thought you might be too late, but she would not tell me what that meant."

"I was in time," the Marquis said.

Nicholas was looking over his shoulder at Harry who was standing a little forlornly just inside the door.

"Stop the Phaeton from driving away!" the Marquis said quickly.

A footman hurried to obey his command and the Marquis said to Harry:

"I think, Harry, you would like to go home in style, would you not? You can drive in the Phaeton and tell your father to come up and see me in an hour or so, and I will explain to him what happened."

Harry's face lit up with excitement and Nicholas cried:

"May I go too? I want to ride in the Phaeton."

"Very well," the Marquis said good-humouredly. "Jason will look after you, and both of you are to do exactly as he says."

"We will be good — very good!" Nicholas cried and he and Harry ran down the steps together.

Watching, Valeta thought how well the Marquis seemed to understand the two small boys and it suddenly struck her that he should have children of his own.

She did not know why, but suddenly that seemed not to be the happy thought it should have been.

Of course it was obvious that he should be married and have a wife to help him entertain in all his fine houses.

"I think, Nanny, we should go home," she said in a voice that suddenly sounded dull and a little bleak.

"Yes, of course, dearie," Nanny agreed.

"I feel that would be a mistake," the Marquis interrupted. "If you will come into the Salon, Valeta, I will explain why."

He did not wait for her reply but walked towards the Salon saying to the Butler as he went:

"Is tea ready in the Orangery?"

"In a few minutes, M'Lord!"

Knowing she must do what he asked, Valeta followed the Marquis only stopping for a second to take off the pretty but inexpensive straw bonnet which the Housekeeper at Stevington House had loaned her.

She gave it to Nanny saying:

"That has to be returned, but I will tell you about it later."

Then smoothing her hair with her hands she walked into the Salon and a footman shut the door behind them.

The Marquis had already reached his favourite place in front of the mantelpiece and he watched her advancing towards him thinking that unlike any other woman he had ever known before she was completely unself-conscious of her beauty.

Valeta reached his side and her eyes were wide and worried as if she expected what he was about to say was something with which she would not agree.

"I think, Valeta," the Marquis said quietly, "it would be wise for you, Nanny and Nicholas to stay here for a few days until we are quite certain there can be no recurrence of what happened this morning."

"But surely now that . . . Lord Lionel is dead . . . ?" Valeta began hesitatingly.

"Cibber is alive," the Marquis said, "and until he has been arrested and put in prison for a great number of years, or transported, I would rather have you safely beside me."

"I had not . . . thought of . . . that," Valeta admitted.

The Marquis did not speak and she went on:

"I kept on feeling grateful . . . although perhaps it was unkind to Harry . . . that Nicholas had not been frightened again by those horrible men."

She shuddered before she continued:

"They had meant to force him into being a climbing boy again, and when they found that Harry was there by mistake, they were going to . . . use him instead."

She gave an involuntary little cry as she said:

"It would have . . . killed Nicholas to have to go through all that horror for a second time . . . I know it!"

"You once asked my support for a Bill to abolish the use of boys in the cleaning of chimneys," the Marquis said, "and I will not only support the Bill, but I will actively campaign to prevent boys being used in any of the houses of my acquaintances."

Valeta gave a little cry of delight and said:

"How can I tell you . . . what it . . . means to me? How can I . . . thank you?"

The Marquis looked at her, then he pulled her into his arms.

"Like this," he answered, and his lips were on hers.

For a moment Valeta was too astonished to think.

Then the Marquis's lips aroused a feeling that she had never known before. It was so strange, and yet so wonderful that she could not struggle or move, but only feel that she had stepped into a dream-world that was more beautiful than anything she had imagined.

The Marquis's lips were gentle, as if she was infinitely precious, tender and yet insistent and she felt as if, though he held her captive, she had no wish to be free.

She felt as if the moment when she had thought he was Sir Galahad come to her rescue, he had been enveloped with the glory that had surrounded the Knight.

He had also the determination of Jason and courage of Perseus, so that all she had ever longed to find in her heroes was there in one man.

The Marquis released her lips and now he was kissing her eyes, her cheeks, her small chin, then again her lips.

It was difficult to breathe as something warm and wonderful moved from her breasts into her throat so that she could no longer speak.

The whole room seemed to be filled with an unbelievable glory and she only knew that if this was love, it was perfect, ecstatic, as she had always known it must be.

Then the Marquis raised his head to look down at her and he said in a voice that she found hard to recognise:

"I love you! I suppose I might have expected this to happen when you came here hating me. But I love you, and there is nothing I can do about it except tell you so."

Valeta's eyes seemed to fill her whole face and the Marquis said with a smile:

"I think I know what you are feeling, as I am feeling the same. It has happened so quickly, so unexpectedly, and yet it is there!"

"You . . . love me?" Valeta asked in a tone of wonder.

"I love you," he replied, "as I have never loved anyone before. In fact, I did not know that love was like this."

"Nor did . . . I," Valeta whispered, "but it is love . . . real love?"

"Very real," the Marquis agreed. "My sweet, I know now that you are everything I want in my wife, everything I thought never to find. How soon will you marry me?"

Valeta's eyes seemed to grow wider than ever. Then she whispered:

"I do not know . . . what to say. You are so . . . grand . . . so magnificent. How could you marry anyone . . . like me . . . ? I think I would be . . . afraid."

The Marquis smiled and it was very tender.

"You need never be afraid of anyone or anything when you belong to me," he said. "That I promise you."

Valeta gave a little laugh that was curiously unsteady.

"I was really . . . meaning I would be afraid . . . of you."

"Not if we love each other," the Marquis said. "I love you, and I want you to tell me that you love me."

Her eyes dropped because she was shy, and he said:

"Oh, my darling, I know it already. I was

aware of it when you came into my arms when I opened the door, and when you trembled against me I knew I had to look after you and protect you for the rest of your life."

"It was . . . so wonderful to see . . . you there . . . when I had been . . . so afraid," Valeta whispered as if she must give him an explanation.

He put his arms round her and drew her close again.

"We have so much to say, so much to learn about each other," the Marquis said.

Then as he pressed his lips against the softness of her skin, he added:

"And you have so much to teach me."

He knew that Valeta was surprised and he explained:

"I have a new crusade: to save the climbing boys, clean up St. Giles' and rid London of much of its crime. Do you think I am capable of that?"

"I think you can . . . do anything you . . . want to do," Valeta answered, "as long as you let me . . . help you."

"Do you think I could do it otherwise?" the Marquis asked. "You have got me into this and now you have to work as hard as I shall have to do. Otherwise I might fall by the way-side."

He was teasing her and she laughed a little tremulously.

"I am so excited . . . so thrilled . . . I do not know what to say."

"Just tell me you love me," the Marquis said. "That is all I really want to hear."

"I do love you," Valeta said, "but I never thought it . . . possible I could do . . . anything but . . . hate you!"

"That is something you will never do again," the Marquis answered.

As he spoke, he kissed her, a slow demanding kiss that seemed to her to draw her very soul from her body and make it his.

Then after a long time when it was impossible to think but only to feel, the Marquis said:

"I had forgotten about your tea. It will be getting cold by now. Let us go and find it in the Orangery."

"I am so happy I feel as if I am disembodied," Valeta said, "and I will never want to eat or drink again."

"I feel the same," the Marquis answered, "but I suppose I have been inconsiderate. I should have given you your tea first, then told you I love you. But when I looked at you I wanted to kiss you so desperately that it was impossible to think of anything else."

He kissed her again before he said:

"Come along. I have to think about you, and you have had a very exhausting day."

"Now it is a very wonderful . . . marvellous day," Valeta whispered.

"If you say things like that and look at me with that particular expression in your eyes," the Marquis said, "you will not only have no tea, but no dinner and no breakfast tomorrow morning!"

Valeta laughed.

"I think the truth is that you want your tea," she said, "so let us go and find the Orangery. I have no idea where it is."

"I will show you," the Marquis said. "There are so many things I want to show you in this house, my darling, a house where we are going to spend a great deal of our time together, for I have a feeling you would prefer living here to London."

"We will have to go to London for you to attend the House of Lords," Valeta said.

"You are already driving me to work?" the Marquis asked laughingly.

"No, only hoping to . . . share it with . . . you," Valeta murmured.

He put his arm round her and drew her towards the door and kissed her again before they went out into the Hall.

The Marquis led her through passages filled with treasures which at any other time Valeta would have wanted to look at, but now she could only think of the man beside her.

The Orangery, with trees that had been brought from Spain nearly a century ago, was bright with sunshine and it glittered on the tea-table set amongst the flowers and beside a fountain in the basin of which swam goldfish.

Valeta looked at the profusion of silver, the silver teapot, kettle, milk-jug, and cream-jug, the sugar basin, all set on a magnificent silver tray embellished with the Marquis's coat-of-arms.

"You must pour out," the Marquis said. "It is something you will have to get used to."

"You are frightening me again," Valeta complained.

But her eyes were soft with love and as the Marquis looked at her for a moment they forgot everything but the enchantment of their feelings for each other.

Then with an effort Valeta poured out the tea and she thought that with the Marquis sitting next to her looking at her as if he had never seen her before, nothing could be more magical, more wonderful than to be alone with him in this beautiful place.

Then there was the sound of footsteps and the Marquis turned his head impatiently as if he resented the interruption.

It was Mr. Chamberlain who came towards them.

"Good-afternoon, Chamberlain!" the Marquis said, "What do you want?"

"I am sorry to interrupt Your Lordship," Mr. Chamberlain replied, "but I thought you would wish to know that a lady and gentleman have called in answer to the advertisement."

"What advertisement . . . ?" the Marquis began.

But Valeta gave a little cry.

"The advertisement about Nicholas! Someone has actually called?"

"A Colonel and Mrs. Standish," Mr. Chamberlain replied. "They live the other side of

London and have been travelling all day since the advertisement appeared in a Hertfordshire newspaper."

"Do you think they are really Nicholas's father and mother?"

"They told me their little boy disappeared when he was playing in their garden. There were some gypsies in the vicinity, and they could only think when the child vanished, that the gypsies had stolen him."

"It said in the report by the Select Committee," Valeta said, breathlessly, "that the gypsies were often accused of stealing children so that they could sell them to the Sweeps as climbing boys."

There was so much excitement in her voice that the Marquis put out his hand protectively to take hers.

"This is only the first answer to our advertisement," he said, "and these people may not be Nicholas's parents. I do not want you to be disappointed if we have to wait for some time to find his real ones."

"What else did these people tell you?" Valeta asked Mr. Chamberlain.

"They said their son was called Nicholas and had a pony called Rufus."

"Then it must be them! It must!" Valeta cried. "Oh, please, darling, let us go and see them."

The endearment had slipped out involuntarily and the Marquis seeing the astonishment on Mr. Chamberlain's face said:

"Perhaps I should tell you, Chamberlain, that Miss Lingfield has done me the honour of promising to become my wife."

Valeta blushed and said in a low voice:

"I . . . should not have . . . said that . . . perhaps you . . . wished to keep it a . . . secret."

"It is no secret as far as I am concerned," the Marquis said, "and I am the happiest man in the world. Congratulate me, Chamberlain."

"You know I do, My Lord, from the very depths of my heart," Mr. Chamberlain said. "And may I, Miss Lingfield, wish you every happiness, which I have a feeling you have both found already."

"We have!" Valeta said. "I did not know it was possible to be so happy."

She looked at the Marquis as she spoke and he smiled at her as if he had forgotten his Comptroller's very existence.

Just for a moment they were both very still, then Valeta said:

"Let us go and see these people, and they must see Nicholas. Where is he?"

"Anticipating that would be your wish," Mr. Chamberlain replied, "I have sent for the little boy and he should by now have reached the Hall."

"Then let us go and find him," Valeta said to the Marquis, "and how wonderful it will be if they really are his father and mother!"

The Marquis took her by the arm and followed by Mr. Chamberlain they walked towards the great Hall.

Nicholas was there playing with one of the valuable bronze ornaments that stood on a table.

"Look," he was saying to a footman beside him, "that is a big lion, and the man is killing it with his spear. Would you like to kill a lion?"

The footman had no time to answer before the small boy saw Valeta and the Marquis and ran towards them.

"I have found a lion on your table," he said to the latter. "Did you ever kill a lion?"

"As a matter of fact I have," the Marquis said, "and when we have time I will show you his skin, but now there is someone I want you to see."

He took Nicholas by the hand and walked towards the Salon.

As Valeta followed she sent up a little prayer in her heart that Nicholas had found his parents.

He was such a dear little boy and she knew that he ought to have a home of his own and people who loved him because he belonged to them.

The Marquis opened the door.

The two people were at the far end of the room, the lady seated in an arm-chair, the gentleman standing beside her.

For a moment no-one moved nor spoke, then Nicholas gave a cry which seemed to echo up to the ceiling and releasing the Marquis's hand he rushed towards them.

"Mama! Papa!"

It was impossible for Valeta to see what happened simply because tears flooded into her eyes.

It was too poignant, too moving and she was conscious only that the Marquis's arm was round her and he was holding her close as if he knew what she was feeling and felt very much the same himself.

Then without saying anything he drew her out of the room back into the Hall and shut the door.

"Let us leave them with their happiness," he said, "as we want to be alone with ours."

He turned to the Butler.

"We will be in the Library if the visitors wish to speak to us."

Walking into the Library he waited until the door shut behind them, then he was kissing the tears from Valeta's eyes.

"Do not cry, my darling," he said.

"They are tears of . . . happiness," Valeta sobbed. "If I had not . . . fought for Nicholas when I came . . . here to see . . . you, and if you had not . . . bought him from that . . . horrible . . . brutal man he . . . would have died . . . I know it."

"I forbid you to think of anything so unhappy at the moment," the Marquis said. "We are happy, Nicholas has found his father and mother, and all we have to do now is to hurry up and have a Nicholas of our own and perhaps some brothers and sisters for him to play with."

Valeta gave a little choked laugh.

"You are going too . . . quickly," she protested.

"There will be plenty of time for us to consider such things," the Marquis replied, "but there is one thing I am not going to wait for, and that is our Wedding Day!"

He kissed her again before he went on:

"Nicholas's father and mother will doubtless stay here tonight and tomorrow I will find another Chaperon for you. But I want you to myself alone, and it would be a bore to have other people with us."

"I, too, want . . . to be alone . . . with you," Valeta whispered.

"As you are in mourning, and I suppose I am too as far as the world is concerned, shall we just be married very quietly and secretly?"

"Could we . . . do that?"

"If you agree, and if you are prepared to be married without our friends gaping at us and receiving a profusion of wedding-presents which neither of us wants."

"How do you . . . know I do not . . . want them?" Valeta asked.

She wanted to tease him merely because she was so happy, but her heart was singing and she felt as if her head was enveloped in clouds of glory.

It was difficult to think of anything but the closeness of the Marquis and the feelings his lips aroused in her every time he kissed her.

"I will give you everything in the whole world you want," the Marquis said, "and throw in the moon and the stars, if you want those too."

There was a deep note in his voice which made Valeta say with her lips close to his:

"I think you have . . . given me those, already."

"Oh, my darling. I love you so much that I cannot think straight," the Marquis said, "and the only thing I want to say is that I love you, over and over again."

He drew a deep breath, then he asked:

"How can this have happened to me so unexpectedly? I never believed in this sort of love before! Yet it is true, it really can happen, that one can find the perfect person to whom one belongs and suddenly the whole world is changed."

"Has that . . . really happened to you?" Valeta asked. "Do you . . . really feel like that about . . . me?"

"It will take me a long time to tell you what I feel about you," the Marquis said, "but it will certainly be easier if we are married first."

He smiled, then his lips were on hers and he felt her respond and knew he had been right when he said this was different.

Never in the whole of his life and his many love-affairs had he known such ecstasy, such wonder and at the same time, a reverence.

He could not explain it.

He only knew deep down in his soul he had always been aware that somewhere in the world there was a woman whom he had not yet met, but who was the right and perfect person for him.

That was why he had never married, that was why despite all his amatory adventures and his raffish behaviour there had been a sacred and untouched shrine within his heart which now in the flash of a passing second had been filled by Valeta.

He knew that in her purity, her innocence, her wise little mind and her compassion for others, she was exactly what he needed in his life — a life that was going to be very different from what he had lived before, and very much more worthwhile.

His lips became very demanding, more possessive and he felt the flames of desire flickering in his body.

Yet at the same time, he knelt at Valeta's feet because she was so different from all the other women he had known.

He took his lips from hers and with a little catch in her voice Valeta said:

"I . . . prayed for you . . . God sent you to save me . . . and He also gave me love. Oh, wonderful, wonderful Serle, our love is so perfect that it is divine, it is a part of God."

And that, the Marquis knew, was exactly what he believed himself.